Finding Joy
in Pain 2

Finding Joy in Pain 2

Roslyn M. Wyche-Hamilton

URBAN BOOKS

http://www.urbanbooks.net

URBAN SOUL is published by

Urban Books
1199 Straight Path
West Babylon, NY 11704

ISBN-13: 978-1-59983-090-2
ISBN-10: 1-59983-090-6

First Printing: April 2010

10 9 8 7 6 5 4 3 2 1

Printed in the United States of America

Acknowledgments

I would like to take this opportunity to extend a warm thanks and my appreciation to all the people who have supported me through my journey. I am blessed to have a God who is there for me through thick and thin. I am everything with You and nothing without You.

I am grateful for my family and my friends for always being there, whether you are reading my book, promoting, encouraging, or supporting. Thank you from the bottom of my heart. To my family—Guy, Jaz and Guy Jr., Mom (Joyce), Mom-in-law (Bea)—thanks for your support. Love you much. Jaz, thanks for staying up with Mommy when she was on a deadline.

Thanks to the people that I forgot to mention in the first book: my brother-in-law Rob H. and my niece Rhonda Wyche. I am so proud of you. Keep up the good work in school! Raquel, Cydney, Taja, Alexis, Nadira, Khiondrah, Sharmasia, Tiffany, Jayanna, and Kira, love you. To my nephews, Khalil (football), every coach's dream and the buzz in South Jersey, and Trevie (basketball), who is going to the number two school in the nation, you are so talented. Keep up the good work. Stay humble. I can't forget my other talented nephew Ajani. I can't wait to see you.

Can't forget Jayvon, Jadus, and Dayvon. To all of my aunties and uncles—love you!

Cindy & Kevin J., Amia F., Renee Gallman-Jones, Nay Nay, Ursula, Onya, Brenda Jean, Tyler, Neddra, Kim M., Lisa G., Amanda, Thurayya, thanks for the shout-out on power 99. Auntie Brenda, thanks for boosting sales in L.A. Dar and Shep, thanks for helping me out with my first book signing. I would also like to thank Lonnie, Mechile, Tee Tee, Kendra, Kahlil W., Mina, Tina, Zena, Lionel, Curtis Bunn-NBCC, Dionne, Monie Love, Trina Stackhouse, Kevin Lomax, and Cyti W.

Additional shout-outs to the lovely ladies of Delta Sigma Theta Inc., the Zeta's and AKA's Between Friends Book Club (Monique, Gi, Rose, Zee, Robin, Lyn, Dar), Neptune Fam, and Del-State Fam. E. Lynn Harris (R.I.P.), thanks for being there when I had questions and for lending your support. You are one of a kind. Thanks to Angel Hunter and Valerie Moore for everything! My gratitude to my agent, Maxine Thompson, and my publicist, Khia Shaw!

Thanks to all the bookstores, book clubs, radio stations, my fellow authors, and my Facebook and MySpace friends. A special thanks to everyone who helped promote my books. If I forgot your name this time, please accept my apologies! I will get you next time.

Chapter 1

After the Wedding

Joi

The ceremony was so beautiful, but after Roc handed me the note about Damon, I didn't know what to think. Jaylen and I had worked so hard to make sure we had the perfect day. I wanted Jaylen to know that my feelings for him were real and heartfelt. When I attended his first wedding, Toni showed every woman there what not to do as a bride. I still couldn't get over the fact that she had read her wedding vows off of a piece of paper. Like I said before, she had just shown up. I hated to say it, but I knew in my heart that their marriage was doomed from the beginning. Toni was fake, uppity, manipulative, and Jaylen was the complete opposite. Now, I knew that opposites attract, but in their case, they retracted.

It was not like we rushed into this marriage. We went to counseling, and we took things slow.

We waited an entire year, because we needed to address our issues openly and honestly. I had made some poor decisions and Jaylen had made some poor decisions from a relationship standpoint. Now that I thought back, maybe it hadn't been such a good idea for me to attend Jaylen's wedding to Toni. There had been just too many unresolved feelings in one room. To make matters worse, Toni's ex-husband, Kenyatta, had been on the same cruise that Toni and Jaylen took on their honeymoon. Now that was just plain old tacky.

Jaylen had found out that the baby he thought was his was not after all. It had been just one thing after another. I had been dealing with the death of my aunt Lex, and in addition to that, Damon had been driving me nuts. But through it all, we had found our way back to each other. There was no doubt in my mind that Jaylen was my soul mate, and I also knew that together, we could get through whatever life threw our way. I know it was not always going to be easy, but we had each other now. So today was the first day of our life together, and the drama had managed to greet me at the door.

My body started to tremble, and I abruptly excused myself from Jaylen and our guests to catch up with Roc.

"Roc? What exactly does this note mean?" I angrily asked.

"Look, Joi, I did not know how else to tell you, but I thought you needed to know."

"So what am I supposed to do now? I can't believe he is out of jail, and now I may be his next target."

"Joi, is everything okay?" Jaylen asked as he entered the room.

"Yes, Jay. I had something important to ask Roc before we left for our honeymoon."

"Well, baby, couldn't it have waited until after we greeted our guests?" Jaylen asked. "You know everybody is asking where you ran off to."

"I'm so sorry, Jaylen. It just couldn't wait. I'll explain everything to you later," I replied.

"Roc, can you please excuse my wife? We have guests waiting," Jaylen said, with an annoying look on his face.

"No problem, man. Joi, don't worry, I am all over it," said Roc.

I knew Jaylen was pissed, but I had to talk to Roc. The note had thrown me into an instant panic. I had so much going on inside my head. For the life of me, I did not understand how Damon could be roaming the streets after all the stuff he did. There was enough proof to convict him of those rape charges alone. What about the stalking charges? Damon is a force to be reckoned with, and as much as I tried to put it out of my head, I knew he was hell-bent on coming after me for revenge. I just knew it. Roc's words played over and over in my head.

Damon was released from jail, and he knows you turned him in, I silently thought to myself. "How am I supposed to go back inside and act like nothing is going on? I can't do it," I said aloud.

I started looking around to see if I could spot Damon. For a second, it seemed like everything around me was spinning out of control. I should have known something wasn't right, because I had this weird feeling inside my stomach. This was supposed to be the happiest day of my life, and now I felt like I was acting out a scene from the television series *Snapped*.

"Joi? Girl, if you don't get your butt back in here. I have been trying to stall the guests until you got back. Where did you run off to? Are you okay?" Faith asked.

"No, Faith, I'm not. Damon was here."

"Here? Where?" Faith asked, with a confused look on her face.

"He was here and Roc saw him."

"I thought his ass was somewhere locked the hell up," she retorted.

"Well, we all thought wrong, because he is out, and it's obvious he is stalking me."

"Look, Joi, there is no way you can go in there and finish greeting the guests. I will let Jaylen know that we have a situation, and I will tell the co-ordinator to make up something. Hey, you can finish making your rounds at the reception, and if the guests don't understand, too bad," said Faith.

I tried my best to put on a smile for our guests, but I was a nervous wreck inside. I didn't know if I should tell Jaylen right now or if I should wait until all our guests left the church. It was obvious that Faith had spoken to the coordinator, because she immediately advised everyone that the bride and groom would continue greeting everyone at the reception facility. Soon after everyone vacated the church, Jaylen took my hand and escorted me outside. Some of the guests blew bubbles at us, and some threw rice. It created the perfect distraction under unusual circumstances. My mother met up with us just as we walked toward our car. She hugged me real tight and kissed me on my cheek. The wedding party had already taken their places in the limousines.

We had a white horse and carriage, which was parked directly in front of the bridal party's limo. The bumper on the carriage had a sign posted that read CONGRATULATIONS TO THE BRIDE AND GROOM. There was an older gentleman standing near the horse, waiting to escort us to the reception. As we made our way toward the horse and carriage, the gentleman opened the door for Jaylen and me to get in. As we pulled off, there was a trail of cars behind the limousines blowing their horns, as we rode off to the reception. The reception was being held at Lucien's Manor, which was an upscale wedding and reception facility. Although, we could have had both the wedding and the reception under one roof, I wanted to have a church ceremony. We were also able to take our formal wedding pictures on the premises. I really did not say much the entire ride. Jaylen held on to my hand and professed to me that this was definitely the happiest moment in his life.

"Joi, you seem to be preoccupied. Is everything okay?" he said.

"Why wouldn't it be? I just married the man of my dreams."

"Well, I just married the woman of my dreams."

Jaylen leaned over and softly kissed me on my lips. I kissed him back, and he just held me during the ride. I wanted so bad to tell him about Damon, but I just couldn't. As long as Jaylen held me in his arms, I felt safe and secure.

"Joi, you have made me the happiest man alive. This just feels so right."

"Jay, I never stopped loving you. I honestly thought I had lost you forever."

"Baby, that's behind us right now. From here on out, it's all about us."

I knew marrying Jaylen was the best thing. I loved his family and he loved my family. My parents had taken him as a son, and his parents had taken me as a daughter. I could see the looks on their faces at the wedding and how happy they were for us. Everything just seemed to be falling in place. However, I really needed to tell Jaylen the truth about Damon and this note before we got to the reception.

"Jay, I need to talk to you about something."

"Joi, you can talk to me about anything," he said while kissing my hand.

"You know back at the church, Roc handed me this note regarding Damon."

I went into my purse and took the piece of paper out and handed it to Jaylen to read.

I tried to reach you earlier to let you know that Damon was released from jail, and that he knows you turned him in. I don't mean to mess up your wedding day. I thought you needed to know. I'm doing what I need to do, so don't worry. I think I saw him here. Be careful.

It seemed as though Jaylen read the note more than once. He stared at it and turned it over, and he looked over at me.

"Roc thinks he might have seen this Damon character at the wedding? Is that why you ran after Roc back at the church?" he asked.

"Yes, Jaylen. I panicked. I'm sorry."

"You should have told me right then."

"I was freakin' out, Jay. One of us needed to look like we were in control to prevent creating a stir with our guests."

"I need to talk to Roc. Is he definitely coming to the reception?" Jaylen asked.

"He's on the guest list, so I have to assume so. Besides, with everything that is going on with Damon, I am almost positive that he will be there."

"Well, let's not focus on this right now. Let me take care of everything. Okay, Mrs. Payne?"

"Okay. I just wanted you to know," I said quietly.

"You're my wife, and it's my job to keep you safe. When Roc gets there, we can talk to him together and get to the bottom of this."

"What if he changes his mind and doesn't show up?"

"Don't worry, baby. I have a plan B. This Damon character may act like he is crazy, but if he tries to bring any harm to you, he will regret the day he was born."

"Well, let's try to put on a united front so that our guests don't suspect anything," I said.

"Will do," Jaylen replied.

We finally arrived at Lucien's Manor. The driver pulled the white horse and carriage up to the front entrance, and the limousines were right behind us. I could see some of the guests walking into the building to attend the reception. The driver put the carriage in park and hopped out. He came around to Jaylen's side and opened the door. Jaylen stepped out and helped me as well. Before we went inside, the coordinator signaled us to a designated area so that we could have our pictures taken. Alongside the building was a landscaped garden with waterfalls and a sitting area perfect for taking photos.

The photographer led the bridal party to one side and Jaylen and me to another. He took pictures, a lot of intimate pictures, of Jaylen and me for about twenty minutes. Afterward, he took pictures of the bridal party, along with Jaylen and me. I didn't think there was a pose he missed. Forty-five minutes later, we headed back into the reception area. It was apparent that the cocktail hour was dwindling down and the guests had already taken their seats. The inside of this building almost blew me away. The entrance opened to a decorative lobby and a grand staircase set under a majestic crystal chandelier. There was imported tile, antique furniture, and classic artwork furnishing the corridors.

"Wow, I didn't realize this place was so nice," Jaylen noted.

"I know. It looks amazing," I said.

"Hey, the best is yet to come, Mrs. Payne."

The coordinator started gathering up the bridal party, including the parents and grandparents. Jaylen and I had to get to the back of the line for the final introduction. The DJ started announcing all the names of the bridal party. My grandparents had flown in from South Carolina to attend the wedding. Jaylen's grandparents were not able to make it, because his grandfather was not in the best of health. We promised them that we would send them a DVD of the wedding. Now it was my and Jaylen's turn to be introduced.

"Ladies and gentlemen, for the second time today, I introduce to you Mr. and Mrs. Jaylen Payne. Now let's give some room so that they can have their first dance," said the DJ.

As we made our way through the room, the DJ had a spotlight on the dance floor. Jaylen slowly guided me to the area of the spotlight and held me close. The DJ played the song we had chosen, which was Jamie Foxx's "When I First Saw You." The song was perfect. I could have danced with Jaylen all night. He saw me crying and started wiping my tears. The rest of the bridal party joined in toward the middle of the song. As I looked around the room, it blew me away. It was so elegant. In one corner there was a beautiful fireplace, and in another corner was a waterfall cascading down a tiled wall. There were marbleized columns adorned with gilded capitals. There was a hand-painted faux sky ceiling, along with ornate crystal chandeliers and eight-foot windows.

The wedding party sat up on a raised dais perfectly situated to observe the room. The pastor blessed the food before we began to eat. After a few minutes, they started serving the salad, followed by the main course. All the guests had a choice of filet mignon, chicken saltimbocca, or stuffed tilapia. I looked over to see how Taj, Eboni, and Gi'ana were doing. Faith was only one seat away, so I was able to talk to her. As Jordan got up, Faith leaned over in my direction.

"Are you okay?" she asked.

"For now. I told Jay everything in the carriage, so we are just dealing with it the best way we can."

"I just can't believe that Damon would have the audacity to show the hell up at your wedding un-invited. Isn't that some type of violation? Is he on parole?"

"It would have been if that was what he was locked up for." I explained. "I mean, he raped and stalked his victims, but he was not charged with stalking me."

"Wow, that bastard," said Faith.

"Can we just change the subject for a minute? I need to clear my head, girl."

"You're right, Joi. I am so happy for you and Jaylen. I saw how you two were looking at each other on the dance floor. Wow, I hope I get that lucky one day and find someone who loves me that much or even half that much," Faith professed.

"Thank you, Faith. I know you will, because you deserve it. I almost lost him once, but I was lucky enough to be given a second chance."

"I see your boy Roc over at the door, acting like security."

"Yeah, that's a long story," I said.

"Are you sure that everything's all right, Joi? You still seem a little preoccupied."

"No, I'm fine," I assured her.

I looked around, and the servers were pouring the champagne so that the guests would make a toast. I felt a sense of relief knowing that Roc was standing near the door. Jaylen's twin brother, Jordan, asked for everyone's attention. He stood up and faced Jaylen and me as he held up his glass of champagne.

"I would like to extend a toast to my brother, Jaylen, and his beautiful wife, Joi. Bro, you most definitely outdid yourself this time. Joi, you picked a good man, too, and I'm not saying that only because we're twins, but because he is the best. You are not my sister-in-law. You are my sister, and you always have been. We love you both, and we wish you a lifetime of love and happiness."

Just as Jordan sat down, Faith stood up.

"Excuse me, everyone. I would like to make a toast. Jaylen and Joi, you make marriage look good. For as long as I've known you two, you have loved one another. Joi, girl, you know we go waaayyy back. I remember when you were a little girl. You used to always say that whoever you married was going to be perfect. Now, I'm not sure if anybody is perfect, but, Jaylen, you seem to be pretty darn close. I love you both so much, and thanks for sharing such a beautiful day with us."

Everybody lifted their glasses to toast the bride and groom. Jay and I hugged Jordan and Faith. I could not help but feel a sense of sadness, because I was thinking about Aunt Lex. She had married Craig, who was the man of her dreams, or so she'd thought years earlier. She put so much into her marriage, and he repaid her by having an affair. To make matters worse, she found out that she had cancer and had to deal with both of those issues. I remember bumping into Craig and his mistress at Red Lobster while Lex was in the hospital, fighting for her life. I couldn't even imagine the agony she had to endure. Through it all, she had her priorities straight, and that was to make sure her son was well taken care of. After she died, it really put a lot of things into perspective. I missed her so much. I just would have liked to have included her in my special day, because I had been a part of her special day. Even though she wasn't here, she was still on my mind and in my heart, and I needed to say something to honor her memory.

"Excuse me, everyone. I would like to say something about someone very special to me, and that is my aunt Lex. I lost my aunt a little over a year ago to cancer, and I know that she is here in spirit. She loved us all so much, and I want her to know that she is my guardian angel. I wish Lex was hear to make us laugh and to be a part of the ceremony. I would like to make a toast in honor of her memory. Aunt Lex, we love and miss you."

After I gave my toast in honor of Aunt Lex, I felt much better. As everyone clapped, Jaylen put his arm around me, and I laid my head on his chest. I truly felt her presence, and that made all the difference in the world.

People were enjoying their food and most definitely the open bar. Some of the guests came up to congratulate us and compliment the ceremony and reception. The DJ started pumpin' some beats, and the dance floor crowded up quickly. Jaylen and I danced with each other off of a few songs. We danced with our mothers, and I danced with my father, as well as with Jaylen's father. My father got a little emotional as we danced to "Wind Beneath My Wings." At one point, I looked over and saw Faith dancing with Roc in a very flirtatious manner, and he seemed to be enjoying every minute of it. Taj wouldn't let Jordan out of her sight. A few times I watched her drag him onto the dance floor. Eboni appeared to be a little annoyed that Roc was paying more attention to Faith than to her. The evening was moving pretty fast and I didn't mind, because I was ready to call it a night. I was emotionally drained.

I was able to spot Miss Daisy Lynn Felton and her husband. Jaylen and I had invited her to the wedding. Ironically, Jaylen had met her on a cruise ship while he was on his first honeymoon, with Toni. While on the cruise ship, Miss Felton had lost all her vacation money playing the slots. Jaylen played the same machine after she got up, and he hit the jackpot. He felt so bad for her that he gave her back some of the money she had lost. She promised Jaylen that she would not gamble the money he had given back to her. Then he bumped into her again, along with her husband. This time Jaylen had lost most of his winnings. Miss Felton had hit the multimillion-dollar jackpot and rewarded Jaylen with a huge amount of money for his act of kindness. They both adopted each other and had kept in touch ever since. She was one of the sweetest people you could ever meet.

I was getting tired, and I could not wait to fall into my husband's arms. Taj and Eboni took turns dancing with Jordan, and Gi'ana danced with her new boyfriend.

Now it was time for us to cut the cake. Jaylen and I both gently put a piece of cake in each other's mouth as onlookers watched. We did not want to make a scene with the traditional smashing of cake in each other's face. I did not feel like fixing my make-up or my hair. Shortly after that, I threw the bouquet. My old neighbor Rhonda caught it with little to no effort. She was so happy and Faith was so disappointed. They both had wanted to catch the bouquet in hopes of getting married one day soon.

"Joi, girl, I was standing right there. How could you miss me?" Faith complained.

"Come on, Faith. Tell me that you don't actually believe that catching the bouquet crap."

"Easy for you to say. You're married now."

"Well, keep on flirting with Roc and maybe you will get married, too."

"Oh, please, girl, he was sweatin' me. I must say, he does look good in that suit."

"Yes, he does, Faith. It seems as though Taj and Eboni both think so as well," I noted.

As we looked over, Taj and Eboni were making their presence known with Roc, and he didn't seem to mind their attention, either.

"Well, we'd only be a substitute for you, Joi," Faith returned.

"And what is that supposed to mean, Faith?"

"Come on, Joi, you're not blind. Roc has always had a secret or not-so-secret crush on you."

"You think so?" I said.

"Uh, yeah. Roc would jump in front of a moving train for you. He protects you like the Secret Service protects the president of the United States."

"Oh, please. He sees me like a little sister. I mean, he has never made a pass at me, and he shows me so much respect."

"If you say so. I guess he has no choice but to move on now, 'cause you's married now." Faith chuckled.

"Happily married."

I looked around the room, and I saw Jaylen talking to Roc. I could just tell by the serious look on Jaylen's face that they were discussing the note that Roc had given me. Jaylen was concerned, and he knew that Roc was familiar with everything that I had gone through with Damon in the past. I had hired Roc to do some private investigation work on Damon because he was acting so strange. He would follow me places without my knowledge. After I told him that I needed my space, he started stalking me. I got so tired of him calling me and cursing me out and then turning around and acting like nothing had ever happened. It was freakin' me out. Damon would e-mail me with crazy poetry about watching me. Shit, I was scared. The icing on the cake was when I discovered information on a cold case in my office and the profile of the suspect fit Damon. I got together with Roc and gave him some incriminating evidence, and Damon was locked up. He had been linked to several rape cases across town, because his DNA had matched up. For the life of me, I didn't know what had gone wrong, but I was sure as hell going to find out when we returned from our honeymoon. I walked over to talk to Jaylen after he ended his conversation.

"Jay, it's time to go. We can let the guests stay and party," I said.

"Your wish is my command. Besides, I cannot wait to get you all to myself."

"What did you and Roc discuss? I thought we were going to talk to him together?"

"Don't worry your pretty little face over that right now. We'll talk about that later. Besides, you had finally let your guard down, and I did not want to spoil that moment."

"What would I do without you?"

"Well, let's hope that you never have to find out."

Jaylen and I walked over to the DJ stand to make the announcement to our guests. The coordinator took over and gave us all our wedding cards, and she put all the gifts in my father's vehicle.

"May I have everyone's attention?" Jaylen said into the microphone. "My lovely wife and I would like to thank you all for coming out to share this special occasion with us. I am stealing her for the evening, but I want you to stay and finish celebrating. Be safe and God bless."

Jaylen grabbed my hand and whisked me away. Roc had a car waiting to take us to the Marriott Hotel. It took about fifteen minutes to get there. We were not scheduled to leave for our honeymoon until the next day. We were already packed to leave for the airport in the morning. Jaylen checked us in, and we headed for the elevator to go to our room. Before I could walk through the door, Jaylen picked me up to carry me across the threshold. After he put me down, all I saw were candles, champagne, and flowers. Out of nowhere, tears started streaming down my face.

"Jaylen, this is so beautiful. Thank you."

"No, thank you for not giving up on us."

"Just hold me for a minute."

Jaylen turned on the CD player, and it started playing "At Last" by Etta James. I just stretched my arms up, and Jaylen grabbed me by my waist.

"Tonight you're all mines, Mrs. Payne."

"Yes, and you're all mines."

"Should I go and start the Jacuzzi?" Jaylen suggested.

"Well, why don't you do that? And in the meantime, I will slip into something a little more comfortable."

"Me too."

I think I saw him here, echoed in my mind.

After slipping into nothing, I slipped into the Jacuzzi's bubbly mixture, alongside my husband. He handed me a glass of champagne, and I finished it off in less than a minute.

"Fill me up again," I said.

"Slow down, baby. We got all night."

"I know, but I just wanted to get rid of this edge."

"That's my job," Jaylen responded.

Jaylen had the music flowing with all our favorite slow songs. I just lay back in his arms without a care in the world. I was so exhausted that I fell asleep in Jaylen's arms while relaxing in the Jacuzzi, but not before we consummated our marriage.

Chapter 2

Our Honeymoon

Joi

The wedding had come and gone, and now we were finally on our way to Jamaica. As much as I wanted to enjoy myself and forget about that note Roc had handed me, I just could not. The fact that Damon had had the audacity to show up uninvited at my wedding was outright disturbing. I wished I smoked cigarettes, because I would be knocking out a whole pack right now. I just wanted to smoke this asshole right out of my head. However, I didn't want to spoil our honeymoon, considering Jaylen's first with Toni had been such a disaster. As I tried to relax, my stomach was doing backflips. I felt like I was about to have an anxiety attack, and believe me, they were no joke. You couldn't breathe, and your heart would flutter ninety miles per hour. It was just crazy, and I was not in the mood to deal with it.

When we got to Jamaica, I was going to soak in the Jacuzzi tub and let the water wrap around my body like a wet, warm blanket.

Jaylen knew how stressed out I was after showing him the note. He was very concerned and pissed off, but he did everything to take my mind off of Damon. Lucky for us, we left for our honeymoon the next morning. We arrived at the Philadelphia International Airport at 7:30 a.m. Our flight on Air Jamaica was scheduled to leave at 8:45 a.m. The flight was about three hours long, and I wanted to sleep through it all, but I needed to be alert. We checked our luggage at the curb and went inside the terminal so that we could personally check in and go through security. Afterward, Jaylen and I made our way down to gate D3. They started boarding the aircraft at 8:15 a.m. There were a lot of people taking the same flight. I wondered if there were other newlyweds on the plane. We stood in line, waiting to board. As I walked past the pilot, I checked him out from head to toe to make sure he looked like he knew what he was doing. He looked well rested and alert.

As we made our way to our seats, I saw several seemingly excited couples on the plane. There was an African American male sitting alone in a window seat, and he stood out. His hair was in dreadlocks, and he was wearing shades. I stared at him from a distance for a good minute to make sure I did not know him. He did not seem inconspicuous, nor was he paying my ass any attention. However, I was definitely going to keep my eye on him, because something about him just did not sit well with me. You never know. That could be Damon in disguise or one of his cronies.

The plane took off as scheduled, and I reclined my seat. I was hoping and praying that we did not hit any turbulence, because I was still not comfortable flying. Jaylen put a pillow behind my head so that I could relax. I wanted so bad to take a little nap, but I refused. I looked over at Mr. Dreadlocks, and he was still sitting in the same position.

Hmmm, that's odd, I thought.

"Joi, are you all right?" Jaylen asked.

"I guess so. I just can't stop staring at that man over there with the shades and dreadlocks. I mean, who wears shades on a plane? What if it is Damon?"

"Calm down, Joi. There is no way in hell Damon is on this plane, and if he was, he would regret it."

"I hope that I am not being paranoid," I professed.

"Not at all. You found out that this dude came to our wedding without our knowledge. Of course that is going to put you on edge. He is probably from Jamaica and is going back home for a visit."

"Well, let's keep an eye on him, anyway, and I am not sharing a cab or shuttle with him, or anybody else, for that matter, because I do not want anybody to know where we are staying."

"Look, Mrs. Payne, as soon as we get back home, we are going to deal with this situation hands on. We are going to find out how he got released from jail. We should be talking about our future together, not about Damon."

"You're right, Jay. Oh, hell to the no, I just know he didn't look over here."

"Babe, calm down. He has every right to look around the plane."

After Jaylen managed to calm me down, we had a heart-to-heart conversation.

"Jay, when you married Toni, did you have any regrets?" I asked.

"Yeah, I had some regrets. I regret not seeing the warning signs early on that there were problems in the relationship with Toni. I regret hurting you by inviting you to my wedding, and I also regret not sticking by you with your career and working things out."

"I can't agree more. You was trippin'." I laughed.

"Aw, man, my biggest regret was letting you go, Joi, and not protecting you, but things are different now. I struggled with that decision. My parents thought I gave up on us too easy. I wanted you back so bad. I tell you, Joi, there were moments that I just broke down because I missed my best friend and my woman."

"Jay, we both made some mistakes along the way. I can't talk. I am still dealing with my big mistake as we speak. Look at me. I have let this bastard take control of my life. This is not me. I just don't know what to do. I'm not weak, but this is getting tired."

"Well, we are not running away from our problems this time. We are going to handle our handle."

"Handle our handle?" I asked.

"Yeah, what's wrong with that?" Jay asked.

"It's ghetto." I chuckled.

"Joi, you think everything is ghetto."

"No, I don't, Jay. It is just annoying when people say, 'To make a long story short' and the damn story gets longer and longer. What about 'It is what it is,' or 'It do what it do'? Please spare me."

"You forgot one, babe. What about 'At the end of the day'!"

We both started laughing, but I still had my eye on Dreads. I knew how to laugh and stay focused at the same time. Jaylen always knew how to take things off my mind, because he kept me laughing all the time.

Just then the pilot's voice came over the loudspeaker. "Ladies and gentlemen, this is your pilot, and we will be landing in approximately five minutes. Please fasten your seat belts and put up your tray tables, and thank you for flying Air Jamaica."

Jaylen and I were looking out the window. We saw what we thought was the beautiful city of Montego Bay. Within ten minutes, the pilot made a safe landing.

"Thank you, Jesus, for the smooth flight and getting us here safe. I just do not like to fly, but I do have to make some sacrifices, and this is one of them," I prayed.

When we decided to go to Jamaica for our honeymoon, we opted to stay in a private villa along the Negril beaches. From the looks of the online brochure, the villa was a perfect spot for our honeymoon. I couldn't wait to see it for myself. After arriving in Montego Bay, we were taken to the shuttle station so that we could be transported to Negril. Dreadlocks hopped on the first shuttle and left with a few others that were on the flight. The shuttles ran every fifteen minutes, so Jaylen and I waited for the next shuttle to come. It took about an hour and a half before we arrived at our destination. The driver removed our luggage, which we had put in the overhead bin on the plane, from his trunk and placed it on a cart. The driver looked like he had not slept in weeks. Dragging his frail five-foot-five, 120-pound frame, he slowly walked back and forth with our bags. His shirt was wrinkled and it reeked of smoke. He didn't seem too interested in striking up a conversation with us. He just wanted to keep it moving. Jaylen gave him a tip and he left.

We were then greeted by a young Jamaican lady, who escorted us to our villa. She assured us that someone would be bringing us our luggage shortly.

As we got closer, we could see the ocean, and it was breathtaking. The water was turquoise blue, and it was so peaceful. I could hear small splashes from the tiny waves lapping along the shore.

"Jay, look at that aqua blue water," I gasped.

"I see it and I cannot wait to get in it. With you, of course."

As we entered our villa, I went into shock. It just could not get any better than this. This villa was very open, with a spacious design, and was fully screened in, with ceiling fans in every room. There was this exotic and lushly planted outdoor walled shower garden. The villa had a designer bathroom with a bidet and a second indoor bathroom with a huge double vanity sink. It had a full kitchen with all the appliances we needed. We were entitled to one cook-service meal per day as long as we bought the groceries. There was a large dining area and a sitting room that opened out into a large, private, open veranda facing the ocean and the beach. The veranda came furnished with a hammock and a swing chair. And last but not least, we walked into the bedroom. There was a romantic four-poster, bamboo, king-size bed with netting and a Jacuzzi. It was just idyllic for couples, and it had that old-style ambiance that we were looking for. I had always imagined us walking along the seemingly endless, stunning beach and the azure waters off the west end of the island. We had wanted to go to a place where we could both just lie back and enjoy ourselves. Jaylen was in need of a relaxing game of golf, and I was in dire need of a hot-stone body massage.

"Can you believe this place? Did I die and go to heaven?" Jay asked in a playful manner.

"This place is unbelievable. I feel like Jill Scott. I'm living my life like it's golden."

"Did you see those beaches we passed on our way here?"

"What is taking so long with the rest of our luggage?" I complained.

After several calls, we finally got the rest of our luggage forty-five minutes later.

"I need another nap. I am so tired from the wedding," I announced.

"You'll have plenty enough time to take a nap, but not right now," Jaylen replied.

"Well, Jay, it's not like I can control not being tired. I just need a minute or two."

"Oh, so you're not going to *obey* me now that you are my wife?" Jaylen chuckled.

"Excuse you. I don't recall saying 'obey' in my wedding vows," I playfully snapped.

Jaylen pulled me close to him and gently kissed me, and I kissed him back. I hadn't noticed earlier that someone had left a bottle of champagne and some fruit in the bedroom.

"Look, baby, somebody left us a bottle of champagne," I said. "That's so nice. They must know we are here on our honeymoon. They even left us a note."

"To the happy bride and groom. Congratulations," Jaylen read.

"That's strange. How does the staff here know that we are on our honeymoon? I never mentioned it. Did you, Jaylen?"

"I really don't remember, Joi. Why are you making such a big deal out of it?"

"Because it is just weird."

"Hey, let's just pop open the champagne. I am sure that they assumed we were on our honeymoon," Jaylen replied.

"Yeah, I guess you're right, Jay."

I didn't want to let Jaylen know how paranoid I was actually feeling. The note from Roc was making me second-guess everything. For a minute, I thought Damon might have sent the champagne just to let me know that he was somewhere nearby. I will be contacting the hotel staff later today to see if they were the ones who sent the bottle of champagne. This whole thing was trippin' me out. I needed to call Roc when I got a chance, because he said that he would do what he needed to do but for us to be careful. How in the hell was I supposed to take that message? He was one of the few people who knew where we were staying, because I trusted him like a brother. So for now, I would let it go. Jaylen and I finished off more than half of the bottle of champagne. A few minutes later, I was starting to feel woozy, so I decided to go and lie down for a few minutes.

"Whew, Jay, that champagne is getting to me. I need to lie down for a minute."

"Now that I have you all to myself, I am not about to let you take a nap. We have some unfinished business to take care," Jaylen replied.

"What unfinished business?"

"We're not finished consummating our marriage."

"You've got to be kidding me. We accomplished that goal last night."

"Well, let's continue where we left off," Jaylen said as he pulled me closer to him.

"You know I can't say no to you, Mr. Payne."

"Hey, you know what they say. No pain, no gain."

Out of nowhere, I felt this weird sensation in my body. I pushed Jaylen away so that I could re-group and get myself together.

"What's wrong?" Jaylen asked.

"It's nothing. I will be okay."

"It's this whole thing with Damon, right?"

"Sorta, kinda. I cannot even relax on my honeymoon, because everywhere I go, I feel like he is lurking around."

"Well, I don't want you to worry your pretty little head over this Damon character. Besides, I took the liberty of getting some extra security."

"What do you mean by extra security?"

"Well, I spoke to Roc the night of our wedding, and we worked something out."

"Okay. I'm waiting. What did you work out?" I asked.

"I hired him to follow Damon and monitor his every move while we are away."

As Jaylen started dialing Roc's cell number, I wanted to see if Roc had any updates.

"Hey, Roc. This is Jay. I was wondering if you could talk to my wife. This whole situation has both of us on edge."

Jay handed me the phone.

"Hi Roc. Jay explained everything to me. I

really appreciate everything you are doing for us. So are there any updates to report?"

"Me and my boy Rick are watching Damon from all angles. So far, so good. I saw Damon driving around town today. I also found out that he was definitely at the wedding. I am not sure of his motive, but I'm working on it, so please enjoy your honeymoon, ma. I'll keep you posted."

"Thanks for the update, Roc. Bye," I said.

"Do you feel better now?" asked Jaylen.

"Oh, Jaylen, that was so sweet of you. Now I can calm down some and enjoy my husband. I just want to know how you two managed to pull this one off."

Roc was like a brother to me, and he knew Jaylen would do anything to protect me. However, he also wanted us to have a memorable honeymoon. I was so happy that I went over and gave Jaylen a big hug and kiss.

"Only the best for my wife."

"You know what we forgot to do?"

"What?" said Jaylen.

"We forgot to open our cards and some of the smaller gifts from the wedding."

"Did you bring all of them?"

I nodded. "Absolutely. I mean, I have to start making a list to send out the thank-you cards. I figured that I might as well do it while we are on our honeymoon, because when we get back, who is going to have time?"

"Well, let's do it."

As I started to go through the cards, I noticed

an envelope with familiar handwriting. If I didn't know any better, I could swear that it was Aunt Lex's handwriting. I took the envelope and sat down over in a corner. As I began to carefully open it, my hands started to tremble. I could tell that there was a letter inside of a card and a small envelope inside of the larger one.

"Jay, it's from Aunt Lex."

"What's from Aunt Lex?"

"There is a card, a letter, and a small envelope inside."

"Do you want me to read the letter for you?"

"No, Jay, I can read it."

I took the letter out and read the card. It was a wedding card addressed to Jaylen and me. I unfolded the letter, and it was three and a half pages long. I took a deep breath before I got started because I knew that no matter what she had put in this letter, it was going to be hard to read.

Dear Joi,

By the time you read this letter, I will have already gone home. I already know that I am dying, and I have finally come to terms with it. I always knew that you two would get back together. You were meant for each other. I could always look in Jaylen's eyes and tell how much he adores and loves you. Sometimes in life we all get off track and lose focus, but I just knew in my heart that you two would find your way back to each other. I prayed for you every day. This is one of the few regrets that I have, besides missing your college graduation,

*and that is me not being able to attend your wed-
ding. So I wrote this letter and gave it to your
mother at the end of May. I asked her to give you
this letter on the day that you and Jaylen got married. Stop crying pleeeaaase. I am okay, Joi, and I
love you. I am so proud of the young woman that
you have become, and I am so happy that you married Jaylen. I also know you were a beautiful bride.
Please tell my nephew that I said hello and congratulations.*

*I was sitting here in this hospital bed, remem-
bering all the good times that we've shared. Hanging out, talking, laughing, hanging at the beach,
standing in the unemployment line (smile), me
trying to teach you how to smoke cigarettes and
watching you choke half to death—sorry, but that
was my way to make sure you never smoked another day in your life, and look, it worked—and
just being the best of friends. Boy, I am going to
miss that and you, of course. Please remember all
the advice that I have given you and always watch
your back, because there are a lot of crazy people out
there. Knowing that Brandon is in very good
hands also makes it easier for me to let go. Believe
me, I wish I could have stayed around, but it's my
time to leave. Always look out for my baby Amelia,
because she is going to need you. I left a letter for
her, as well as for everybody else that I needed to.
Boy, my hand is tired. Please don't be angry with
Craig, and please forgive him, as I have.*

*I wanted to get you something nice, but I was a
little low on funds. I mean, I obviously can't work*

and make money if I'm stuck in this hospital, so I want you to have the necklace that I put in the smaller envelope as a keepsake. I hope that you like it. It's my way for us to stay close, and I can also watch over you. Please share it with Jaylen from time to time so that I can look out for him, too (smile again). I am going to miss you so much, as well as the rest of my family, especially Brandon, but I am so proud of him. Please don't cry. I am ready to go. I know that I will be in a much better place. Always thinking of you! Stop by to visit me whenever you can. I love you, niecy. Congratulations and always keep God first!

Love,
Auntie Lex

"Baby, are you okay?" asked Jaylen.

Sniff, sniff. "Yes, Jay, I am. She wrote this letter three weeks before she died."

"She was a special person," Jaylen said.

"Yes, she was and I will always cherish it."

"She knew that we were going to get back together."

"Yeah, she did. She loved you, too, Jaylen," I told him.

"Are you going to put on the necklace?"

"I would love to. Can you help me latch it in the back?"

"No problem, baby."

Chapter 3

Let's Have Some Fun!

Joi

Jaylen put the necklace around my neck. I walked over to the mirror to see how it looked, and it was beautiful. It had a heart-shaped pendant with five diamonds on the right side. It made me feel close to Aunt Lex, and it also made me think of the day we lost her. Somehow her death had brought Jaylen and me back together. He was there for me when she died, and we never left each other's side from that point on. She knew how much Jaylen's marriage to Toni had devastated me, and she was there for me through it all.

"Are you sure you are okay?" Jaylen asked.

"Actually, I am feeling better. Let's go out and walk around."

"I'm ready when you are."

"I know that you want to go and play golf, so can you teach me how to play?" I asked.

"You must have read my mind."

I could see Jaylen's face light up. He changed into a pair of beige shorts and a white polo shirt. I changed into a pair of light blue capris and a matching shirt. I threw my hair up into a ponytail and put on a hat and some shades. Jay also put on a baseball cap and some shades to block the sunlight. We went outside to wait for a cab to take us over to the golf course. I told Jaylen that I wanted to rent some mopeds so that we could go riding around the island. I saw so many people riding them, and it was fun. I had a moped when I was younger, and it was like riding a motorcycle. It beat riding a bike. I wanted the flexibility to ride around town and get a good look at the island. It was hot outside, and you could see the schoolchildren dressed in full uniform. I guess they were used to it. We passed a Shell gas station, which was pretty cool. The familiarity made me feel at home. For the time being, I put all the drama with Damon behind me, and it felt good.

We finally arrived at the golf course fifteen minutes later and walked inside of the building to rent some equipment and shoes. Jaylen purchased two packs of golf balls for us to play with. We put our golf clubs into the golf cart, along with a couple of waters, and drove off to our assigned hole. I knew I would not be able to play eighteen holes, so we agreed to play only nine. Jaylen put this little stick into the ground and placed a ball on top and stood next to it. He swung his arms back and hit the ball as far as he could. Next, he moved me up to the area designated for women. He showed me how to put the stick into the ground and place the ball on top. He told me not to swing at it like it was a baseball, but to spread my legs. Jaylen told me to keep my eye on the ball and follow through. I did everything he told me, and I failed to touch the ball. After numerous failed attempts, I hit the ball a few feet to the left.

"It's okay, Joi. That was good for a beginner."

"Whatever, Jaylen. I suck."

"Yeah, but just a little." He laughed.

"Hey, I don't exactly see Tiger Woods out here," I replied.

"Point taken. Now let's walk and grab your ball, and then we can hop in the cart and drive to mines," he said.

"Cute, real cute, but that's okay, because once I get a hold on this game, watch your back," I warned.

We continued playing the holes. I improved my swing with each hole. At the eighth hole, I hit the ball straight into the water. Of course, Jaylen's ball made it over. It was so relaxing and actually a lot more fun than I had expected. After we were finished, we returned the equipment and headed back so that we could take a shower and relax before going to dinner.

"So do you have anything planned for us later on?" I asked.

"I made dinner reservations for us tonight at seven."

"What is the name of the restaurant?"

"It's an evening cruise where they have dinner and dancing."

"Oh, that sounds nice, Jay."

"I also have a little surprise for you when we get there," Jaylen announced.

"That is so sweet. You know I love surprises. I guess I'm going to have to give you my surprise when we get back."

"You don't hear me complaining, Mrs. Payne."

"I bet you're not going to. Oh yeah, I took the liberty of scheduling us both for his and her massages tomorrow afternoon. I figured we can go and soak up some sun and have a few fancy drinks. You down?"

"Whatever keeps a smile on that beautiful face. Besides, I am in serious need of a massage," Jaylen replied.

We returned to our private villa, and when we walked inside, there was a dozen beautiful red roses in our bedroom. The note with the bouquet read: *To my beautiful wife. I love you. Always, Jay.*

"Oh, Jay, baby, you didn't have to send me roses. Just kidding," I said, smiling ear to ear.

"I am going to spoil you every chance I get."

"You know I can get used to this."

"I want you to."

"Thank you. So do you want to join me in the shower?" I asked.

"I think you already know the answer to that," Jay replied in a sexy tone.

"Sit back on the bed. Let me give you a little show while I am getting undressed."

"Wait. Let me get some singles."

"Ooh, Jay. You are so bad. This is for your eyes only."

I went over to the entertainment center and put on a song by Maxwell. I started dancing for Jaylen as I undressed. He never took his eyes off of me. I could tell that he was really turned on. After I finished undressing, I walked over to him and pulled him up off of the bed, and I started undressing him as well. Afterward, I led him into the shower. The water was nice and steamy. As I stood in front of Jaylen, he lathered up my entire body with soap. I returned the favor. We both stood under the water to rinse off the suds. Jaylen took it upon himself to lift me up against the shower wall, and it was on at that point.

We started kissing, and we both were wet from head to toe. He kissed every part of my body until I was unable to contain myself. We made love in the shower for almost an hour. We finally made our way back to the bed. I lay in Jaylen's arms and we fell asleep. At 5:00 p.m. we were awakened by the alarm clock. I was so tired, and I hit the snooze button on the alarm because I needed at least another fifteen minutes. It felt like I dozed off for what seemed like thirty seconds, but it was actually fifteen minutes.

"Come on, baby, we have to get up now. The

dinner cruise leaves at seven, so we need to leave here no later than six fifteen," Jaylen reminded me.

"I know, but this bed is just so comfortable," I moaned.

"Don't worry. We'll got out tonight but tomorrow I plan on buying some groceries and making you a nice candlelight dinner. I already made arrangements to have the cooks whip us up a nice breakfast spread outside, overlooking the hills."

"Okay, it's really time to get up. What are you wearing?" I asked.

"Hmmm, I figured that I could wear that white linen pants outfit you packed for me."

"Good choice. I will wear my white linen dress," I announced.

We got dressed in about thirty minutes, but I still had to figure out what I was going to do with my hair, since it got wet in the shower.

"Jay, what should I do with my hair?"

"You're asking the wrong person. It looks nice the way you have it now."

"I didn't do anything to it. It just dried up from the shower."

"Whatever you decide to do with it, you are going to have to make it quick, because our ride will be here in ten minutes."

"I didn't even put on my make-up yet," I groaned.

"Put it on in the car. We have to go in a few."

I put some mousse on my hair and brushed it back as fast as I could. I decided to twist my hair up into a bun. I grabbed one of my white flower hairpins and placed it over the top of the bun.

"How does my hair look, Jaylen?"

"You look like you belong on *America's Next Top Model*."

"I will take that as a compliment. By the way, you don't look too bad yourself."

Our cab arrived and drove us to the dock where the dinner cruise was located. There were a lot of people waiting in line to board. I noticed a lot of couples who looked like they were also on their honeymoon. After we boarded, we were escorted to our seats. There was a lady and a man walking around with tropical drinks. There was island music playing in the background, and a few of the couples decided to get up and start dancing before we left the dock. I was still a little tired from playing golf all day and spending some quality time with my husband. However, I was excited about this dinner cruise, and I was also very hungry. Finally, the boat sailed off into the sunset. We ate, drank, and danced off of fast and slow music. We really had a good time. Jaylen could see that I was tired, so we walked out on the deck and sat down. I laid my head on his chest, and we talked until I fell asleep on his shoulder. A little while later Jaylen tapped me on the shoulder to let me know that we had docked.

"How long was I asleep?" I asked.

"For about an hour or so."

"Jay, I'm sorry. I didn't mean to fall asleep on you."

"Hey, as long as you were here in my arms, sleeping, I did not mind."

"Wow, how did I get so lucky?"

"No, I'm the lucky one. I told God that if He gave us another chance, I would make sure I was the best husband I could be. I don't ever want to take you for granted. I just want us to put our past behind us and move on to bigger and better things."

"I am on the same page. I know I pushed you away, and I will never do that again. We both ended up in some pretty crazy relationships, and I do not want to ever go back there again. I mean, once we get everything handled with Damon, we can keep it moving."

We arrived back at our villa. Jaylen gave the cabdriver a tip, and we went inside and got ready for bed. Jaylen held me close all night long.

The next morning we got up, and the staff had prepared our breakfast. We showered and threw on some clothes and ate everything from bacon, eggs, sausages, and French toast to pancakes, grits, and fresh fruit and had whatever beverage we desired. We were stuffed. We had his and her massages scheduled for noon, so we ran out to the straw market for a few minutes because I wanted to pick up some souvenirs for my family. I also wanted to buy some Jamaican liquor and wine for my collection. The straw market had a little bit of everything. Most of the vendors were women, and some were children. We walked from one end all the way to the other end.

"Excuse me, how much are your T-shirts?" I asked.

"Dem tree for ten dollars," a woman answered.

"That's not bad. I would like to buy six," I told her.

"Wut size?"

"Two medium, two large, and two extra large."

"Dat will be ten dollars."

Jaylen was at another section, buying some key chains. I went over to see if there was anything else that I needed.

"Babe, why are you buying those little key chains?" I laughed.

"I'm just picking up some for the people at my office. You know they have been really working hard during these tough times, and this is just a small token of my appreciation. Once I get things back on track, I plan on giving them a nice bonus."

"Well, baby, I wish that you would let me help out. I have a nice stash put away."

"So do I, Mrs. Payne. Remember the money Miss Felton so generously gave me? I still have that to fall back on, and I would rather put that to use under extreme circumstances. If I get this big account with the city, I will be better than fine."

"When do you expect to hear anything on your bid?" I asked.

"Hopefully soon. I've made some contacts, so I don't want to jinx it."

"I understand."

After we left the straw market, we arrived right on time at our appointment for our massages.

"How may we help you?" the receptionist asked.

"Oh, we're here for our massages," I said.

"Your names please?" she asked.

"Jaylen and Joi Payne," I told her.

"Oh, you're right on time. Please follow me to the back," she said.

As we started walking to the back, the young woman told Jaylen to go into the men's dressing room to put on the robe, and she also showed me the women's dressing room and advised me to do the same thing. We were both instructed to lock up our belongings in the lockers. Afterward, we had to meet up in another room, where they had cool beverages waiting for us. Jaylen poured us both a glass of pink lemonade as we waited. Finally, after about seven or eight minutes, two women came by to escort us to a room in the back. They stepped out of the room after asking that we remove our robes and place ourselves under the sheet on each bed. As Jaylen took off his robe, I could see every muscle from his shoulders down to his feet. He was lucky we didn't have a few minutes, because it would have been on and poppin' in that room. I was so caught up in looking at him, I forgot to take off my robe, and it was so obvious.

"Baby, you need to hurry up and take off your robe before those two come back," Jaylen advised.

"Oh, you're right. My mind just drifted off."

"To where?" Jaylen teased.

"Don't start, Jaylen. This is not the time or place." I laughed.

"You know you can always come over here and get under the sheets with me."

"As much as I would love to do that, I'll pass."

As I dropped my robe, I could feel the sexual tension in the room. Jaylen reached out his hand to grab me, but I moved away. I slid under the sheet just in the nick of time.

Knock, knock.

"May we come in?" called one of the masseuses.

"Yes, you may," I replied.

At first, they adjusted the music in the room to ensure that we could hear it. The music playing was peaceful and serene. Jaylen and I faced each other since our beds were side by side. They began by easing one leg out from under the sheet at a time. The masseuses inserted hot stones between each of our toes. It felt so good. Afterward, they started rubbing warm oils along our inner and outer thighs, followed by hot stones, which hit every inch of our legs. They switched over to our other leg to repeat the process. I could tell that Jaylen loved every minute of it. I caught him almost falling asleep on two different occasions. They continued to massage our arms, and then they asked us to turn over so that they could continue with our backs. They massaged our backs with the hot oils, but when those hot stones hit my back, I gasped.

"Oh, that feels so, so, so good. I don't want to get up no time soon," I said.

"Baby, you are definitely going to have to learn how to do this," Jaylen replied.

"Well, if I learn how to give you a hot-stone massage, who is going to give me one?"

"How about we learn together?" Jaylen suggested.

"Now you're talking," I retorted.

The massages were finally over, and we got dressed, checked out, and left. It was so refreshing. I felt like a whole new person. Jaylen and I went back to the villa to change into our beachwear because I was in need of a serious tan. I wore a black bikini, and Jaylen put on some black shorts and threw a towel around his neck. I got caught up in the ambiance and threw on a beige straw hat and some Dolce & Gabbana shades. I dug through my luggage until I found those cute black sandals to accentuate my bathing suit.

"Wow, look at you. Are you sure we are going to the beach and not to a fashion show?" Jaylen asked.

"I'm just having a *How Stella Got Her Groove Back* moment," I revealed.

"Oh, that's what you call it," Jaylen teased.

"Well, you are my groove, and I did get you back."

"That was cute."

"Is it too much, Jay? Because I will change."

"No, you look gorgeous. My baby can't help it if she is a diva."

"Look at you. You look like you're ready to rip the runway," I teased back.

We finally packed a bag, which included books, iPods, sunblock, sandals, towels, and our camera. We had a semiprivate beach, and only the people who were staying in the villas were allowed to enter the premises. There was also a pool with a couple of bars in the immediate area. As we walked down onto the beach, Jaylen spotted a really nice area for us to relax and get some sun. After we got settled in, we rubbed sunblock on each other to avoid sunburn. We ordered a couple of rounds of drinks, placed our iPods in our ears, and lay back. It couldn't get any better than that. I was listening to Tina Marie and Luther Vandross oldies, and Jaylen opted to listen to the O'Jays and the Whispers. After about an hour had passed, we got up to go in the water. Words could not describe the color of this water. It looked like something you could just jump into and drink at the same time. I jumped on Jaylen's back, and he walked me around like we used to do in college. After swimming, we walked back to our chairs, and then we ordered a couple of turkey burgers with cheese, along with an order of fries.

"Would you like to order another drink?" the waiter asked with a Jamaican accent.

"May we just have some water with lemon? We've already had two drinks, and we are not trying to get tipsy," I replied.

"So what are we going to do when we get back to our villa?" Jaylen asked.

"I am going to sleep, Jaylen. I am beat."

"I know that you are, but don't forget that I am cooking you dinner tonight in our private little villa."

"That would be so nice. I just need at least four hours of sleep, and then I will be ready for any- and everything."

"Well, I will make sure you get your proper rest," Jaylen promised.

"I would suggest the same to you, because I cannot wait to make love out on the beach tonight."

Jaylen could not believe what I had just said. He wasn't complaining. He just did not expect to hear me say that for some reason. I'd always wanted to hold hands and walk along the beach, but only with Jaylen. He meant everything to me.

"Jay, are you blushing?"

"Girl, men don't blush. We just smile."

"Whatever," I said while smiling.

"Well, I look forward to tonight."

"I got the perfect dress to wear, and believe me, I don't have to take it off for it to be off."

"What in the hell kind of dress is it?"

"Just wait and see for yourself."

We went back to the villa, and as I walked in, I noticed a beautiful arrangement of blue roses on the table. Jaylen walked into the bedroom to change his shirt.

"Oh, Jaylen, you are going to make me cry," I called.

"Why would I make you cry?"

"For everything you do to make me happy."

"You're my wife, and it's my job to make you happy and protect you."

"Thank you so much. I just hope we stay like this forever."

"If and when we have a glitch in our marriage, we will fix it together. For better or worse. Divorce is not an option. When we turn one hundred years old, I am going to bring you back here and say, 'See, I told you. Still together.'"

"Wow, I don't think I will be interested in coming back here when I am a hundred years old. Let's just focus on us right now." I laughed.

"Did you open your card?"

"Oops, I'm sorry. Let me see what it says," I rambled.

I opened the card, and there were twelve massage gift cards from Toppers Spa near our home, one for each month of the year.

"I don't know what to say," I said. "You are incredible, Jaylen. You didn't have to send me flowers. The gift cards were more than enough. Now, hold that thought, because I didn't come empty-handed."

"What flowers? I didn't order any flowers," Jaylen said as I ran into the bedroom to get my gift for him. "You didn't have to get me anything. You know I don't care about stuff like that."

"It's just a little something that you need. Here, open it up."

Jaylen took the gift bag and pulled out a box. He opened it up to find a 100 percent genuine leather, engraved attaché/laptop case. It was dark brown, and under the flap it said JAYLEN P. in small lettering.

"This is just what I needed. I had planned on going to the mall when we got back home to purchase another one. When did you get this and how?"

"That's none of your business, baby. Just know that I got skills," I replied.

"Thanks, Joi. You are the best wife any man could ask for," he said while giving me a kiss.

"You are welcome. Now that we have that out of the way, I am going to go and lie down. Let me know if you need some help in the kitchen."

"Well, actually, I did want to talk to you about those flowers. I didn't send them, Joi."

"So how did they get here, and who are they from?" I said, looking quite confused.

"Joi, before you panic, let's read the card first, before you start jumping to any conclusions."

I looked on the bouquet and found a small card, which read *Congratulations*. There was no name on it, so I started getting nervous again.

"There is no name on the card," I squeaked.

"Maybe one of our family members sent them," Jaylen said.

"I doubt it. Why would they not include their name? That does not make any sense. First, the mysterious bottle of champagne, and now these mysterious roses. Look Jaylen, I need to know where all this shit is coming from. I am going to go speak to the hotel manager to see if they can tell us something."

Jaylen and I immediately went to the hotel lobby and spoke to the manager. He contacted the florist, and they could not confirm any specifics at that time because there was a language barrier. The only person who spoke English had stepped out, so we would have to wait until they returned. As for the bottle of champagne, it had been sent to the wrong honeymoon suite, according to the manager. We offered to replace the bottle as a courtesy, but the manager explained to us that it was not necessary. Frankly, I did not believe him, but what was I going to do? I needed more information about the flowers.

After we returned to our honeymoon villa, I dove into the bed and snuggled under the sheets. I must have fallen asleep within minutes, because I did not remember anything. I woke up several hours later and took a shower. Jaylen had prepared a delicious dinner by candlelight, accompanied by a bottle of wine. We ate, talked, and laughed. He refused to let me help him in the kitchen because he wanted me to save my energy for later on.

By 10:30 p.m., we were on the beach, holding hands. The weather was still warm, and there was a hint of a breeze grazing us as we walked and put our feet in the water. As much as I was enjoying this moment, I thought about the situation with Damon. Jaylen asked me a question about marriage, and I didn't hear him.

"Joi, you didn't answer my question."

"I'm sorry. I was just thinking about something," I told him.

"I hope it's good thoughts."

"Me too. Jay, can we talk for a minute?"

"Sure. About what?" he said.

"About us. I mean, I am having the time of my life with the man of my dreams, and I am scared of losing that. You know as well as I do that marriage can be tough."

"I hear what you are saying, but what a lot of couples do is fail to communicate. They take each other for granted, and some were never ready for marriage to begin with. We put God first in our life, and that makes all the difference in the world. You know in your heart that we were always meant to be, and not everybody can say that. Whatever problems we face, we face together. We both come from two strong families who have strong marital bonds."

"You are right. I can't argue with you on that. I mean, what happened to my brother, Wil, could have torn apart a marriage, but my parents worked and prayed through it together, and look at them now. Still together. Well, I promise to do all that, plus some. Let no weapon formed against us prosper," I preached.

"Do you feel better now?"

"Yes, I do. Now let's go play in the sand."

I started running from Jaylen and he scooped me up and we went over to a secluded area. I lay back on a light throw, which Jaylen had grabbed from our villa. I unsnapped the front of my dress, and Jaylen soon discovered that I had absolutely nothing on underneath. If only we had a video. The lovemaking we shared that night would definitely go down as some of the best. I actually wore Jaylen out, because he passed out and slept for over an hour. I woke him up and we went back to our villa. I was not sure if there were other people on the beach, but I really did not care. I was on my honeymoon.

The remainder of our honeymoon was great. We took so many pictures, and I couldn't wait to set up my honeymoon photo album. As much as we were enjoying ourselves, it was time to get back home and start our lives together. I had taken a total of three weeks off. I needed that extra week to regroup after we returned home.

A few more hours before we headed to the airport the manager at the flower shop contacted the manager at the hotel and advised him that those blue roses had been ordered via the Internet. Some of the information was blocked, which made it harder to find out who had sent them. With Jaylen, I was ready to face anything, whether it was good or bad. I didn't have to take on the world by myself.

Jaylen made arrangements for the hotel to come and pick up our luggage at our private villa. The shuttle service was scheduled to pick us up and take us to the airport. After going through all the security checks, we were ready to board our plane. We were able to wait in the front of the line because we had arrived early. We made our way to our seats and sat down. I just laid my head back and turned on my iPod. Lela Hathaway's remake of Luther Vandross's song "Forever, For Always, For Love" was playing softly in my ears. She was one of the few people, and I did mean few, who could sing the hell out of a Luther song. Just as I opened my eyes, I noticed that same dude with the dreadlocks was on our plane.

"Jaylen, did you just see what I saw?" I asked while nudging him.

"Yes, dear, and maybe it's just a coincidence."

"Look at his ass. He has a laptop. I bet you he did not come here to visit relatives, because he ain't even Jamaican. He's another Jafakin'. I'm going to go and feel him out."

"No, you're not, Joi. Leave that man alone."

"He probably is the one who ordered those damn flowers off the Internet. It all makes sense to me now. The hotel said that they were ordered that way, but the contact information was blocked, so the florist could not tell who had ordered and paid for them."

"Joi, now you are going overboard."

"I'm just going to ask him what time it is."

"Whatever, Joi. It's not like I can stop you."

I walked over to where Mr. Dreadlocks was sitting. He still had those damn shades on. He kept reading whatever magazine was in his hand. I just figured that I would ask him some silly questions.

"Excuse me, sir. Do you have the time?" I asked.

"Yeah, it's time for you to get a watch," Mr. Dreadlocks said.

"Excuse you?"

"Just kid-ding. It 'tis five after ten."

"Tank you, sir."

What a fake. He started off speaking American English and ended the conversation in Jamaican English. I couldn't believe how sarcastic he was toward me. Nothing about him looked familiar. He was a light brown–skin brother with dreadlocks and a tattoo of a snake on his right hand. I could not see his eyes, because he kept those shades on his face. I really did not pick up any crazy vibes, which was a good thing, but you never knew.

Chapter 4

Back to Reality

Joi

Honk, honk.
"I can't believe all of this freakin' traffic. I've never seen it like this before. This is crazy."

Cars were everywhere, and people were blowing their horns out of frustration. I wondered what the hell was going on. I was trying to pull my car over to see if I could get a peek, but to no avail. People were starting to turn around in the middle of the street in an effort to avoid the traffic jam. I had no choice but to stay in this mess. I had promised Faith that I would meet her for lunch today at noon. I had just got back from my honeymoon a week ago, after being gone for two long, wonderful weeks. Ooh, I was still feeling good, and I refused to let this traffic delay spoil my mood.

"I'm just going to block this mess out."

Luckily, Faith was my girl, or otherwise, I would have nicely turned my car around in the middle of this street and jetted. It would be a wrap. I needed to call Faith and let her know that I was running a little late. She had made reservations at this new restaurant called Champagne's on Market Street. It was located in the Old City part of Philadelphia. Supposedly, the food at Champagne's was the best around.

"Damn, where is my cell?"

As I was searching in my pocketbook for my phone, the passenger in the vehicle behind me started blowing his horn out of control.

Honk, honk, honk, honk.

What the hell is wrong with him? I wondered.

It wasn't like I was holding him up, because we were moving only five miles per hour, if that. He was so lucky that I had just got back from my honeymoon, because we would have started a road-rage war. However, I decided to just let it go and take the high road. I was so happy right now, and I would not relinquish any of my positive power for anything.

I finally found my cell phone and dialed Faith's number.

"Hello?"

"Faith, it's me, Joi."

"Hey, girl. Where are you at?" she asked.

"Stuck in traffic on Market Street. Are you at the restaurant?"

"Yes, I am. I heard that there was an accident on Market."

"Well, it's going to take me a minute to get there," I said.

"Are you near Fourth or Fifth Street?"

"I just passed Fifth Street. Why?"

"Make a U-turn and go down to Fourth Street and then make a left. Stay on Fourth all the way down until you see South Street, and make another left. Take South Street all the way down until you see Third Street, and make another left. You'll see a parking garage on your right. Park your car there and walk two blocks, and you will see the restaurant on your right."

"Okay, so basically make a U-turn, three lefts, park the car, and walk two blocks, and Champagne's is on the right. Right?"

"Yes, Joi. Now hurry up so you can fill me in on all the details from the honeymoon."

"I know you are not trying to be all up in my business."

"Well, you don't have to tell me everything." Faith chuckled.

I made the U-turn and sped through the traffic light. Just barely making the light, I could see some of the cars behind me and in front of me making U-turns as well. I followed Faith's directions, and I made it to the designated parking garage within minutes. I parked my car and proceeded to walk two blocks up the street.

Old City was best known for its historical flare. It looked like a combination of the 1800s and modern times. There were tour buses everywhere, and the tour guides were dressed like Ben

Franklin. Some of the side streets were made of cobblestones, and the tourists were riding in horse carriages. Old City had a lot of restaurants with outside seating. On any given Friday or Saturday night, the streets were filled with people looking to barhop or to find a club to party. It was also located within minutes of Penn's Landing and South Street. A lot of younger people walked up and down South Street, which had a lot of clothing stores, eateries, hair-braiding salons, and so forth. There were police officers patrolling the corner streets because it could get a little crazy sometimes. Penn's Landing was more family-oriented. They had a lot of free concerts and festivities for the children. People took the ferry over from New Jersey to visit.

Anyway, I was just glad I didn't have to walk two blocks on these cobble streets with these high heels, because my feet would start hurting me. I had only one more block to go, and even though I didn't particularly like walking in heels, I wanted to soak up this historical atmosphere. I just wanted to continue enjoying the scenery.

I stopped briefly in front of a soul-food restaurant called Soulfully Delicious and read the menu that was hanging in the window out of curiosity. They had all my favorite foods, and the prices were reasonable. If I weren't meeting Faith, I would have definitely stopped in for a quick lunch. A young black male opened the restaurant door and looked me up and down.

"Will you be dining with us today?" he asked.

"Oh no, not today. I was just checking out your menu," I told him.

"Well, please come back and dine with us another time. We have the best food and best prices around," he said.

"Wow, is that everyone's claim to fame?" I thought.

As I proceeded to walk away, I thought I heard someone call my name from behind.

"Joi?"

As I slowly turned around, I didn't see anyone. "I must be hearing things," I muttered to myself.

Out of nowhere, the same strange feeling that I'd had at my wedding invaded me. I started having flashbacks of Damon. As hard as I tried to put him out of my mind, unpleasant thoughts of him kept resurfacing.

"I'm just hearing things," I said, convincing myself.

I finally made my way to the restaurant. As I opened the double glass doors of Champagne's, I could see Faith sitting over at the bar. I must admit, Faith had good taste. This place looked like something out of an upscale magazine. I just hoped the prices were not too steep.

"Hey, girl. It's about time you got here. I thought I was going to end up having a liquid lunch," Faith said.

"Please. I was taking my time and soaking up the city."

"Yeah, I know what you mean. I love coming out to the free concerts on the Pier, shopping, and eating. They had Angie Stone and Carol

Riddick a few weeks ago. I went to both and had a ball."

"Well, you could have asked me to come with you, Faith," I remarked.

"Joi, please. You were too busy getting ready for your wedding."

"You're right. Things were hectic, but it was all worth it," I said, smiling.

"Oh, do tell. Do tell."

"I am not going to talk about my honeymoon, standing here at this bar. Where is our table?"

"We have a table. I was just waiting for you to get here. But I figured that I would stand at the bar because I noticed a couple of cuties in here, and you know a sistah like me has to get her flirt on," Faith insisted.

The hostess came over and escorted us to our table. We both ordered raspberry-peach iced teas. There were sliced peaches in our drinks, and they tasted really good. I took the peaches out with my spoon to eat them; but they were frozen. The waitress made her way back to our table and took our order, and no sooner than she walked away, Faith jumped right into question mode.

"So, how does it feel to be married?"

"It's a good feeling. I mean, a really good feeling."

"So, is your sex life better? I mean, like, is there this deep connection that you share afterward?"

"Dang, Faith, don't hold back. That is none of your business."

"Well, Mrs. Payne, inquiring minds like me want to know."

"Look, Faith, you are my girl, my roadie, my dog, but I am not gonna sit here and talk about what me and my *husband* do in the bedroom. Emphasis on *husband*."

"Oh, you wifey now, so I guess you'll be saying, 'My husband this and my husband that.'"

"Okay, Faith, since you are like my sister, I will tell you a little somethin', somethin'."

"Whatever," Faith said.

"He is amazing in so many ways, and he took really good care of me on our honeymoon. I mean, I was jumpy, and at times I could not relax, but Jay was very attentive to my needs. He made sure he did something for me every day while we were on our honeymoon."

"Like what kind of stuff?" Faith asked.

"Wait a minute. I'm getting to that part. You know, just little things with big meanings. He gave me an engraved key with our names on it because he said I will always have the key to his heart."

"Wow, Joi. How far should I stick my finger down my throat?"

"Stop hatin', Faith. I bet if it was Tyree, you would be making it a big deal."

"That was a low blow. I am so done with that situation. I have truly moved on, so go on and continue with your story please."

"I'm sorry, Faith. I wasn't trying to upset you."

"Oh, girl, please, I'm done with that. So again, let's move on," Faith said.

"Well, I got twelve gift cards to go to my favorite

spa each month of the year for a massage. Jaylen took me to this beautiful restaurant on the water, and after we ate, we danced for hours. He had roses delivered to the room every day. Well, with the exception of one day, but I don't want to get into that. You know, just thoughtful things, because he just wants to make me just as happy as I want to make him."

"Wow, you guys were just meant to be from day one. I'm so jealous. I hope I can find someone who can make me happy like that. Some of these dudes out here are off the chain."

"Well, maybe you should be a little more careful with your selection process," I said.

"And what is that supposed to mean, Mrs. Payne?"

"Well, you kinda did meet Tyree over the phone after you dialed the wrong number," I reminded her.

"That could have just been fate," Faith said.

"Yeah, well, in this case the wrong number led to the wrong man. That's all I'm saying."

"Well, well, well. Now, Joi, you are my girl, and I love you like a sister, but let's not go there. I see I need to remind you of a few things."

"Like what, Faith?" I asked.

"Like Damon. You met him in a legal environment, and it turns out that this brother has some real legal problems. That's all I'm saying."

"Touché," I retorted.

"No, seriously, Joi. Is there something that you are not telling me?"

"Well, actually, there are some things that I have not brought to your attention about Damon."

"Like what? And why not?" Faith snapped.

"Well, remember at the wedding I followed Roc out of the church?"

"Yeah, I remember. You told me that Roc saw Damon at the church."

"Anyway, a lot of strange things have been happening to me. Like a mysterious bottle of champagne showed up in our villa. We thought it was a gift from the hotel, but they said it was delivered to the wrong villa. I also received a dozen blue roses, which Jaylen never sent."

"You are blowing me away with all this. Do you think that Damon somehow found out where you were going and had that stuff sent to you to freak you out?"

"Ah, yeah. You think?"

"Is there anything that I can do?" Faith asked.

"No, girl, Jaylen is all over it. He is a godsend. In spite of all my paranoia, he is just being so patient and understanding. I can't let this run my life."

"You need to go and get a restraining order, Joi."

"Look, enough talk about Damon. I came here to kick it with my dudette, so for now, the hell with Damon."

"On that note, let's eat," Faith replied offhandedly.

The waitress arrived with our food, and we said our graces and started to chow down. I ordered a petite filet served with shrimp scampi, roasted potatoes, and broccoli. Faith ordered stuffed salmon, wild rice, and mixed vegetables.

"Okay, girl, enough about me. How is the new job over at the hospital?" I asked.

"I love it. It can get a little crazy, but then again, I am over in the mental health/psychiatric ward. I deal with a lot of outpatients, so all I focus on is their files. I make sure I read through them to prepare me for what I am up against prior to my meeting the patients."

"Are there any patients that you know?"

"Not really, but even if I did, we have a strict confidentiality rule in my department and with the hospital, period. The money is good, and I'm not trying to lose my job for no one."

"Okay, fall back. You're getting a little extra hyped over some damn departmental protocol at your job, and at the end of the day, I understand. I deal with the same sorta thing."

"It does suck at times, but it pays the bills."

"Point well taken," I said.

We finished up our food, and Faith grabbed the bill. It was nice of her to treat. We finished filling each other in on what was going on with Taj and Eboni. We got up to leave, and Faith offered to take me to my car.

"Did you park in the garage that I told you to park in?" she asked.

"I sure did."

"Do you want me to take you to your car?"

"No, girl, I'm straight. I can walk to my car in ten minutes. Plus I need some fresh air."

"Joi? What if he was the one who sent that bottle of champagne and those blue roses? What in the hell does a blue rose mean? I'm going to have to Google that one. You know that I Google everything."

"Hey, I'm not sure what the hell it means, but when you find out, let me know. I only know what red, white, pink, and black mean," I said.

"Are you absolutely sure, Joi, that I can't drive you to your car? I can't believe you are this comfortable walking all around Philly after what happened at the wedding."

"Look, Faith, I just can't let Damon run my life. I have to do this. Besides, it's not like he would take time out of his schedule to track me down."

"Are you sure about that? All I'm saying is that if he thinks you turned him in, then you never know."

"I mean, I hear what you are saying, but why would he want to bring any more negative attention to himself? That's just stupid."

"Okay, suit yourself. Just call me as soon as you get in your car," said Faith.

"I will. Don't worry. Smooches."

When I left the restaurant, I felt a new sense of strength. I was determined to regain my independence. As I made my way back to my car, I could hear my girl Beyoncé's new song "Diva" playing in my head.

"Na, na, na, Diva is a female version of a hustla, of a hustla, of a, of a hustla," I sang.

I stopped singing the song as I approached the soul-food restaurant. The same young man waved to me from the window, and I smiled and waved back. I kept on walking, and I heard someone call my name just as plain as day.

"Joi?"

As I turned around, Damon was standing directly in my face. My new sense of strength suddenly became my new sense of fear, and the smile that I had on my face instantly faded.

"Damon? Uh, hi. Um, what are you doing down here?"

"Wow, babe, you act like you just seen a ghost. Did I frighten you? You lookin' good," he said, looking straight through me.

"W-why would you frighten me? I just didn't expect to bump into you out of nowhere. So how have you been?" I said, sounding choked up.

"I'm good. How about you?" Damon asked.

"I'm good, too. Well, it was nice talking to you, but I have a meeting and I'm late."

I started walking away, and Damon grabbed my arm and pulled me back.

"Get the hell off of me, Damon! Don't you ever grab me like that, or so help me, I will press charges so fast," I yelled.

"Calm down, Judge Hatchett. You dropped something, so I was just trying to be nice and pick it up for you. That's what I get for being a nice guy." He smirked.

Damon handed me a business card. I was so nervous, I just grabbed it and put it in my pocketbook.

"Nice guy, my ass. You stay the hell away from me," I growled.

I quickly turned back around and crossed the street. I immediately reached into my pocketbook to grab my cell phone, but I could not find it. I realized at that point that I must have forgotten it at the restaurant.

"You're welcome, Mrs. Payne, and by the way, congrats on your recent nuptials. I wish you the best. I heard you were a beautiful bride. Jaylen is a lucky man." He laughed out loud.

I tried to play it cool, but my mind was saying, *Run, bitch! Run!* I wanted to turn around so bad to see if he was following me, but I just couldn't. I needed my cell phone, but I was not going to turn back around to go get it. I finally made it to the parking garage entrance. Just then Faith drove up.

"Joi, what took you so long? You left your cell phone at the restaurant, and I know you go nutso if you don't have it," Faith said.

I couldn't focus on what she said, because I could not believe what had just happened. My mind was in a state of shock.

"Joi, what's wrong, girl? Why do you look like you just seen a ghost?" Faith asked.

"You're not going to believe this, but guess who I just ran into while walking back to my car?"

"Who?"

"You'll never guess in a million years."

"Well, as long as it wasn't that nut Damon, then who cares?"

"Well, you'd better start caring, because that nut is here in Philly," I said.

Faith could see that my whole body was shaking, so she jumped out of her vehicle. "Oh, my gosh, Joi, did he threaten you or hurt you?"

"Not really. I mean, he grabbed my arm really tight but claims that he was just giving me something that I had dropped. He was just acting kind of weird. But what's even crazier is that I could have sworn I heard somebody call my name earlier, on my way to the restaurant."

"What do you mean you heard someone call your name earlier? Did you see anybody or look around?" Faith asked.

"Well, actually I did look around, but I didn't see anyone, so I did not make a big to-do about it. On my way here I heard the same voice call my name, and when I turned around, he was standing an inch behind me. That shit was scary as hell."

"Girl, we need to call the police because there ain't no way in hell he just ran into you out of nowhere. This dude is a stalker and he is dangerous. Get in my car. I'll drive you to your car in the garage, and I will follow you home. Do you need me to call Jaylen?"

"No, I'll call him in a minute," I replied. "I need to catch my breath. Thanks for being here. There was a reason why I left that cell phone at

Champagne's, because God knows I needed you, or else who knows what might have happened."

"Well, I know that you are married to your cell phone just like me. So when I saw that you left it on the table, I immediately left the restaurant."

Chapter 5

Bittersweet

Joi

I finally made it to my car. As I was driving, I called Jaylen and told him what had happened. He did his best to keep me calm on the telephone, but it was obvious that I was pretty upset.

"Baby? I will be home in fifteen minutes," he assured me. "I'm leaving work right now, so don't worry. I'll beat you home. He is not going to hurt you. I'll see to that."

"Okay, Jaylen. I'll see you at the house. I'm better now that I've talked to you. Besides, Faith is following me, but I'm going to tell her to get off at her exit. As a matter of fact, she is calling me, so let me click over."

"I love you."

"I love you, too, Jaylen."

Click, click.

"Hey, Faith."

"I am just checking on you. Did you talk to Jaylen yet?"

"Yeah, I just hung up the telephone with him. He's leaving work as we speak, and he is on his way to the house. He will be there in fifteen minutes, so he'll beat me home."

"Do you need me to follow you home just in case you get there first?" Faith asked. "You know that I will."

"No, I can handle this myself. Besides, I can't let Damon freak me out like this. He just caught me off guard. Now I'm ready for his unexpected bullshit."

"Okay, Ms. Superhero. Just make sure no one is following you after I turn off. I don't care if it is a cab, bus, motorcycle, car, or bicycle. Watch your back."

"Thanks for your concern, Faith, but I'll be all right. Stop worrying."

"Girl, please. Do you watch *Snapped* or *Americas' Most Wanted*?"

"Not really," I responded.

"Well, ya need to, because they have everyday nutcases on that show who are off the chain. I watch all of them, including *Forensic Files*, because if a man is going to try and kill me, it's going to be a little difficult."

"Damon may have issues, but he's no killer."

"You don't know what his capabilities are. Stop acting so naive. Damon is a straight nut."

"Okay, Faith. Thanks for being concerned, but I will be all right."

"Well, I got your back if you need me," Faith said.

"And what are you going to do, Miss Badass?"

"Uh, don't get it twisted. You heard some of my poetry. I don't play when it comes to the people I care about, and you're my best friend and just like a sister to me. I mean, we may argue and disagree, but that's what sisters do."

"Awww, that is so sweet. I love you, too. Now you're going to make me cry."

"Joi, please. You'd better put up those emotional walls and stay focused. I'm calling Roc as soon as I get home."

"For what?" I asked.

"I want him to know what happened today."

"Whatever."

"Girl, please," Faith said.

"Okay, play dumb all you want. You know that you like Roc."

"No, Joi, I do not like Roc."

"Roc is a good man and he is very protective. He would be good for you," I said.

"Yeah, and your point?"

"Well, my point is that Jaylen asked Roc to keep an eye on Damon while we were away, and he did."

"Wow, now that's a good husband and a good friend," Faith declared.

"Faith, Roc is a keeper. Don't wait and slip up, because you know Taj and Eboni both have been checking him out. But I know for a fact that he is interested in you."

"Point taken. Roc is not necessarily my type. I just never really thought of him in that way. I mean, we flirt a little here and there, but it is harmless."

"Well, all I'm saying is that you need to let this man be your rock and rock your world. He can be your rock of love."

"Something is seriously wrong with you. You are watching way too much reality television. So does that mean Jaylen is your pain in the ass?"

"Whatever, Faith." I laughed.

"Everything that you are saying may be true, but he is a private investigator," Faith snarled.

"So what's the problem?"

"That means he is probably nosy as all hell, and I can't have some man all up in my business like that."

"That's ironic. You don't seem to have a problem when you are all up in my and Jaylen's business," I noted.

"That's different."

"How, Faith?"

"I don't know. It just is." She chuckled.

"Well, let me go because *my husband* is waiting for me."

"Call me later, girl," Faith said.

"I will."

As I got out of my car, Jaylen met me outside. I went up to him and he gave me a hug.

"Hey, Jay, thanks for coming home early."

"I wouldn't be anywhere else. Let's go inside. I've already made some telephone calls, and I found out where Damon works out. He also works as an independent personal trainer."

"Where?" I asked.

"Body-Liscious," Jaylen said.

"Body-Liscious?"

"Yeah, I know the name sounds crazy, but it's that new gym where a lot of actors, models, and professional athletes go to work out. It's over in Burlington. I'm going over there tomorrow morning."

"Jay, please reconsider. Damon is not worth it, and besides, there is no telling what he might do if he is pushed. He was just trying to intimidate me."

"I'm not going to just sit around and do nothing. He needs to be shut down. My job is to protect you, and that's exactly what I plan to do, with or without your blessing, baby. Now, I'm going to attempt to make myself real clear for him when I tell him to stay the hell away from you, but if he tempts me, we may have a bigger problem on our hands."

"Don't stoop to his level. He's not worth it," I insisted.

"Did he say anything to you that you're not telling me?"

"Not really. I told you everything that happened. I mean, he just gave me back a business card that I supposedly had dropped."

"What card? Did it have any personal information on it? Let me see it."

"Okay, Jaylen, please calm down. You're making me nervous. One of us has to be the calm one."

Jaylen shook his head. "You're right and I'm sorry. I just don't want anything to happen to you."

As I reached into my pocketbook, I pulled out

the card that Damon had supposedly picked up for me, and it read ROC DAVENPORT—PRIVATE INVESTIGATOR. The strangest thing was that I had never seen this business card before, nor did I need it, because I knew Roc's number by heart. Now I was starting to feel uneasy again.

"He knows, Jaylen," I said while handing him the business card.

"He knows what?"

"Damon knows that I hired Roc to check him out. He must have dropped the card with the intention of giving it to me to let me know that he was on to me. I've never seen that card before in my life. He must be trying to send me a message."

"We may need to go down to the police station and file a restraining order," Jaylen said in an adamant tone.

"Okay. Well, right now I have a headache, and I need to go lie down."

What a day. Jaylen wanted to go and get a restraining order on Damon, and I just didn't know if I was ready to deal with all this. I had become the poster child for stalked women. Jaylen just did not understand that every time something happened to me and it involved Damon, it hurt my career. The more I pissed Damon off, the more he came after me. I wished that I had never met him. Things had started off nice, but as time had gone on, he'd started changing. It was like he became obsessed. He had always been aggressive, even when we'd had sex, and he would get mad when it was time for me to leave. Everything had been about scoring a touchdown, which was equivalent to him coming. He was as strong as an ox and he knew it. If I had acted as though I wanted to get up from the bed, he would tackle me back down. Having sex with him had been a challenge, and it would leave me exhausted. He could go for hours. At one point I had thought he was on steroids. One thing was for sure, I had learned my lesson.

Chapter 6

Don't Judge a Book by Its Cover

Faith

Boy, work was going to be crazy today. I didn't sleep much at all. Between running to the bathroom all night and worrying about Joi, I was beat. I hoped I didn't have food poisoning, because that was the last thing I needed. I'd never had a problem eating salmon before, but that was what I got for trying new restaurants. I hated to vomit, because it was disgusting and it left this nasty-ass taste in your mouth. The back of my throat was sore and scratchy.

I yawned. "Whew, let me jump in the shower before I am late for work. I just got this job, and I can't call out sick, even though I really am. Hmm, maybe they will tell me to go home or to the emergency room."

That thought went out the window when I thought about how it would affect my paycheck. I needed every penny to get through these hard times. I wanted to start saving some money, but I was not too comfortable putting my money in the bank. Every time I turned around, companies were shutting down or financial investors were running off with your life savings. The stock market was bipolar, because investor confidence was all over the place.

I was so glad that all I had to wear to work was a uniform. I had forty-five minutes to get to work, so I needed to get ready fast and in a hurry. After I got out of the shower, I put on my uniform, brushed my teeth, and fixed up my hair. Everything else I needed, I just threw in a bag until I got to work. Luckily, my job was only fifteen minutes away, because if it was farther, my ass would be in trouble. I made it to work just in the nick of time. As I went to get a cup of tea, my supervisor, Francis, was turning the corner right in my direction.

"Good morning, Francis," I said.

"Good morning to you, Faith. Are you okay?"

"Yeah, I just have a small case of food poisoning."

"What did you eat?" she asked.

"Salmon."

"That'll do it. You have to be careful with seafood. It can mess you up."

"I see."

"Well, go and get your tea, because we got one busy morning, and you have two new patients."

"Two new outpatients?" I asked.

"Yes, you do, and they are both a piece of work."

"How do you know that they are a piece of work? I thought they were new."

"They are new to you, Faith. Not to us. They've been coming here for a long time. We had to reassign them to you, but don't worry." She chuckled.

"I guess I'd better get my tea, so that I can be relaxed and focused."

"Please, Faith, all the tea in China won't get you through this." Francis chuckled again.

It was bad enough dealing with one new patient. Now I had to deal with two. I was so glad that I had taken those additional courses in behavioral disorders. I had thought Francis was going to tell me to go home or to go down to the emergency room to get checked out. After getting my tea, I grabbed the files of the new patients so that I could become familiar with who and what I was dealing with. My first new patient's name was Delores Grant, and her file was so thick. She was on her way from seeing the psychiatrist in our department. Afterward, I would check her vital signs and pinpoint any other possible health ailments. It was our job to make sure the patients got proper medical attention. Well, it was not as easy as it sounded. These patients would take you through it. They'd scream and spit if they got upset. I had one that tried to bite me. You just never knew when they were going to flip out on you. Before I had a chance to familiarize myself with the file, the patient was in the waiting room.

"Faith. Delores Grant is ready to see you," the receptionist announced.

"Thanks. She can come in," I replied.

As I assisted the patient in the examination room, she just stared at me with these huge brown eyes. She didn't say anything. She was a frail woman who looked like she had been through some things. Most of her teeth were gone, and her hair was gray. You could tell she had been a looker back in her day, but the streets or something else had got the best of her. That was my assumption, but I really didn't know. Ms. Grant just looked like she'd lived a hard-knocks life. I gave her a hospital gown and explained to her that I needed her to change.

"Who in the hell are you?' she asked.

"My name is Faith, and I am the nurse who is going to give you a checkup, and after I get done, the doctor will come to finish."

"Bitch, please. Don't talk to me like I'm some crazy-ass old woman. I know what the hell I need to do," she yelled.

"Okay, Ms. Grant, please calm down. I'm not trying to upset you. Would you like some water?"

"I don't want any damn water. I want some Hennessy. Can you go down to the liquor store and get me some? Can your lazy ass do that?"

Whew. I had to stop for a second and regroup, because this lady was off the chain. I knew she was just testing me, so I had two choices. I could either put up with her outbursts or control the situation.

"Look, Ms. Grant. I will not listen to any more outbursts from you. I said go in the room and put this gown on so that we can do our job and take care of you. Do you understand me?"

"That's all you had to say. I just wanted a drink."

"No drink."

"Can you go and get my son?"

"Is he out in the lobby, waiting for you?" I asked.

"He'd better be."

As she went to change, I asked Francis to tell Ms. Grant's son that his mother was requesting him in the back.

"Oh, she always says that," Francis noted. "Her son is not here. She gets transported to and from home by transportation set up through the hospital."

"Poor lady. No wonder she acts like that."

"Hey, don't judge a book by its cover. That lady might be crazy, but she probably has more money than you and I put together."

"How do you know?" I asked.

"I saw her house before. Apparently, her son is some big-time hotshot, and he purchased that home for her a few years back. But from what I hear, he barely visits her, and she has no other family. She lives there all alone."

"What a shame," I said.

"Yeah, but what can you do? We asked her if she wanted to consider living in an assisted-living facility, and she said that she did not need any assistance."

"I guess she was confused."

"I guess so. I mean, we took her on a tour and let her meet some of the residents. She said that she couldn't leave her son, because he needs her. Go figure," Francis said.

"What is her son's name?"

"Who knows? At one point she said his name was Stevie Wonder."

"Wow. She actually said his name was Stevie Wonder?"

"Yeah, but she is just talking to be talking. Shit, last week her son was Jamie Foxx. It changes all the time, but she is just lonely. Once you get to know her, your perception of her will change. Believe me, we've all been in your shoes. But, don't let her fool you. She is smart as a whip. I think she just likes coming here because she gets to talk and drive us crazy."

"Do you think his name is in her file?" I asked.

"I already checked and I didn't see a thing. I am just as nosy as you." Francis laughed.

"I am not nosy. Why does everyone think that?"

"One day just go with transportation to drop her off. Just say it is for medical reasons. I'll sign off on it."

"For real?"

"For real," Francis answered.

As I made my way back into the room, I found Ms. Grant just sitting there, staring at the blank wall. Her mind seemed to be so far away. I had to call out to her several times before she responded.

"Ms. Grant?"

"Yes, Henry," she whispered.

"Who's Henry?" I asked.

"Oh, he is my dear friend. Henry?"

"Ms. Grant, Henry is not in here."

"Well, isn't your name Henry?" she snapped.

"No, Ms. Grant, my name is Nurse Faith. Let me check your vital signs."

After I gave her a checkup, she put her arms around me so tight, and she started to cry. I didn't know what to do, because for some reason she touched my heart.

"Please don't leave me. I just don't know what I'd do," she cried.

"I'm not going to leave you, Miss Delores. Can I get you some juice and crackers?"

"You know what, Henry? I thought you was coming back home to see me."

"I'm not Henry. I am Nurse Faith." Maybe she thought I looked like a man or something.

No, she is just a little touched, I thought to myself.

Miss Delores could care less what I had to say. As far as she was concerned, my name was Henry. It seemed as if she had had a bad experience in her past, and it had just set her off. She cried for over an hour. After the doctor saw her, transportation came to take her home. I helped her get herself together, and she just looked back at me and smiled.

Chapter 7

Losing Control

Joi

I couldn't believe I was back at work, and they wasted no time in piling up my desk with these crazy-ass cases once again. Every time I took a vacation, no one did any of my work. It just sat around. Now I had to reorganize my desk before I could move on. I didn't know where anything was at.

"Damn, this will take me all day. There is over three weeks' worth of work to go through. Who in the hell put all these lunch menus on my desk?"

It was obvious that I was in a bad mood, because my emotions were all over the place. I was stressed the hell out. This whole thing with Damon was taking its toll. This was not the way I wanted my marriage to start out. Then again, the note from Roc at the wedding had really shaken me up. The honeymoon had been great under the circumstances. Still, that extra bottle of champagne had sorta, kinda initially freaked me out. I felt as though I was holding back from giving my all to my husband. On the other side, Jaylen was doing everything in his power to hold it all together for me, but it was so hard. I kept having nightmares, and I was not eating or sleeping right. Jaylen took it upon himself to go and tell my family some of what was going on, and now everyone was worried. This entire situation was out of control. Maybe I just needed to go down to Damon's job. I mean, this could all be a big misunderstanding. I would have liked to think that I knew Damon well enough to see where his head was at. I needed to get down to that gym before Jaylen did. I was going to call Taj to see if she would come with me. I wanted to tell Jaylen, but then again I didn't want to tell him, because he would just try to talk me out of it.

"Hello, Mrs. Payne. Welcome back and congratulations," the receptionist said when I stopped at her desk on my way to the break room.

"Good morning, Cindy. Thank you."

"Is there anything that you need for me to get you?"

"Not right now, but can you tell me who was sitting in my office while I was away?"

"Nobody that I can recall. It's been a madhouse around here."

"Why do you say that?" I asked.

"Well, Veronica went out on maternity leave earlier than expected, Rich broke his nose playing football, the computers were down for two whole days, and—"

"And nothing, Cindy. I have heard enough to last me for an entire week."

"One more thing. The police finally arrested that doctor who shot his ex-girlfriend out in Cherry Hill."

"Yeah, I saw the file on top of my pile. I'm going to have to read over this one after I straighten out my desk."

"Well, it's really good to have you back."

"Thanks, Cindy. I'm just not sure I want to be back."

I grabbed the newspaper in the break room. I needed to read to clear my head a little before I tackled my desk. I turned the pages to the matrimony section to see if our wedding had been mentioned in today's paper. It should have been listed sooner, but they'd misplaced our photo, so they promised me that it would be in there today. As I started looking for our wedding announcement, it was clear to me that it was not in today's paper. However, just as I started to turn the page, what did I see? There was a picture of Tyree and Cre'ole, announcing their recent nuptials. I could not believe it. I didn't know if I should be mad that my and Jaylen's picture was missing or shocked to see Tyree and Cre'ole. There was no way I was going to tell Faith. She would have an absolute fit. I knew she said that she was over him, but I could just tell by our conversation the other day that she had not completely forgotten him.

"Now I have a headache," I quietly complained as I walked past Cindy's desk with the newspaper in my hand.

"Would you like some Motrin, Mrs. Payne?"

"No, Cindy. I have some, but thanks, anyway."

"Okay."

"Wow, that girl has some super ears. How in the heck did she hear that?" I thought, *If she responds to that, her little ass is outta here. That will drive me insane.*

After returning to my office, I went into my purse and grabbed some Motrin. After popping two of them into my mouth, I continued reading the newspaper.

"I am going to call that newspaper and give them a piece of my mind," I said, sounding frustrated.

I couldn't help but notice a picture on the front page of the sports section. It was a side-shot photo of some local high school athlete named Marcus Taylor. From the looks of the picture, he had slam-dunked the basketball in three of the players' faces on the opposing team. Watching our youth doing such positive things absolutely made my day. Just growing up in today's society was so rough. There was so much pressure out there with all the gangs, drugs, and murderers. Just to see some positive press helped balance out all the negative stuff we read about in the news-paper, in magazines, and on the Internet.

"You gotta love it," I muttered to myself.

"Mrs. Payne, I took the liberty of bringing

you a cup of coffee just the way you like it to your office."

"Oh, Cindy, you are the best. What would I do without you?"

"Well, let's hope that you will never have to find out."

Cindy was the best receptionist and assistant you could ask for, and she was only twenty-one years old. She was a pretty girl with strawberry blond hair that came down to her shoulders. She loved to wear the latest fashions. She reminded me of that girl that played the lead actress on *Gossip Girl*. However, she could be over the top, and at times it was annoying. She had graduated from Harris School of Business with a degree in paralegal studies a little over a year ago. She had come with high recommendations from her instructor Kia Wash, who was a good friend and colleague of mine. Her goals included going to college and eventually law school. She was always asking me a lot of questions about becoming an attorney, and I just tried to guide her in the right direction.

Anyway, the coffee was just what I needed to get me out of this funk. I had not talked to Taj or Eboni since I'd got back from my honeymoon. Both of them had called me several times, but I had not gotten around to calling back yet. I needed to call Taj, anyway, to see if she would go with me down to the gym where Damon worked.

Ring.

"Hey, Taj. What's up, *chica?*"

"Well, it's about time you returned my calls, diva," Taj replied.

"I know, girl, but you know how it is. I'm just trying to get settled in, and with all the Damon bullshit, it's just been crazy."

"Girl, I heard. Faith filled me in. Yo, what's up with that dude?"

"Who knows? But Jaylen is not trying to hear it. He wants to go down there today and confront him. I just figured that it might be better if I reached Damon first, so nothing crazy jumps off."

"Are you serious, Joi? Let Jaylen handle that situation. He can handle Damon. Besides, he can take that sexy-behind twin brother of his with him and double-team his ass," Taj said.

"Look, Taj, I need to get down there immediately. Are you down?"

"Down with what?"

"I need for you to come down to Body-Liscious with me to confront Damon," I explained.

"Hell to the no! You have truly bumped your head. Next, he will start messing with me, and right now I am focusing on my modeling career."

"Girl, I need you. Jaylen wants to file a restraining order against Damon because of what happened in Philly last week. Although I do understand where he is coming from, hopefully me confronting Damon will work instead. I just want to avoid the whole restraining-order issue for now, Taj."

"Joi, you are playing with fire, and I ain't tryin' to get burnt."

"Okay. I understand. I just thought you might like peeking at all the eye candy professional athletes who work out there."

"Ooh, Joi, that is low. What time are we going?" Taj laughed.

"Now. I am on my way to pick you up, so be ready."

"Wait, Joi. I need at least thirty minutes."

"For what?" I asked.

"I look a mess. I need to change and do my hair and make-up. You got your man. Hell, you got two men. One caught you, and the other one is still chasing you."

"Cute, Taj. I will give you fifteen minutes. That's it."

"Since you put it that way, I'll just sling on a wig with some booty shorts."

"Uh, don't forget to put on a top and something on your feet," I teased.

"Ha-ha. You're real funny. I might be desperate, but I am not stupid."

Beep. "Mrs. Payne, your husband is on line two. Should I take a message?"

"No, Cindy, I will take it."

Click.

"Okay, Taj. I have to go. Jaylen is on the other line. I'll be there in fifteen minutes. Please be ready when I get there."

Click.

"Hello, Mr. Payne."

"Well, hello, Mrs. Payne," said Jaylen.

"So what's up?"

"Nothing much. How is your day going so far?" he asked.

"Well, you know I was a little stressed out, but I'm good right now. How is your day going so far?"

"I am a little busy, but everyone at the office pretty much handled things while I was away."

"I wish that I could say the same thing about my office. I have so much work on my desk. There is no way I am going to be able to get much of anything done in this lifetime."

"Just try to take it easy. That work is not going anywhere, so do what you can," Jaylen said.

"You're right, but my OCD just kicked in, and it is driving me crazy."

"Well, I just called to check on my beautiful wife. I have to go and take care of some business today, during lunch. I'll see you at home. I love you."

"Love you, too, Jay. I have to ask you something. Are you still going down to the gym at lunchtime to speak with Damon?"

"Yes, baby. I am. I know you may not be comfortable about me going, but everything will be fine. I'm not trying to jeopardize my livelihood over this knucklehead."

Now my day had just got that much crazier. I guess I had to get used to being married and having someone other than my girls to lean on. I still had to beat Jaylen down to the gym. In a way it felt good to have someone in my life that had my back. I just wanted to try to control the situation to make sure it did not boil over. When I thought of what Jaylen and I had been through, all I could do was count my blessings, and all this stressing out that I was doing was just a waste of energy. I needed to call my mother and see what she was up to.

"Hello, Mom. I was just thinking about you, so I wanted to give you a call."

"You must have read my mind, because I was just about to call you to see what was going on with you and Damon."

"It is nothing for you and Dad to worry about," I assured her.

"Well, tell that to your father, because he is about to take matters into his own hands, and there is nothing that I can do to stop him."

"Please tell him that Jaylen and I have it under control."

"Yeah, I know, but after everything that happened to Wil years ago, he vowed that he wasn't going to let anybody bring harm to this family again, and he meant that."

"What is it that he plans on doing?" I asked.

"Oh, you know your father. He won't do anything crazy. He'll just make a few phone calls, and that's that."

"Well, Mom, I just wanted to call and check in. Can you please tell Gi'ana to call me later on this evening?"

"I sure will. I love you."

"Love you, too, Mom."

I needed to go out and get some fresh air. I had not been able to do any real work, because of everything that was going on. The last thing that

I needed now was having my father involved. I just wished Jaylen had not told my parents anything. However, my dad was a reasonable man with a lot of connections. He was well respected by so many people in the community and church, and especially by his family and friends. I had never disclosed my situation regarding Damon, because I did not want him to worry. The only person I had confided in within my family circle was Aunt Lex, but now she was gone. I needed to go and find Damon right away. I had to squash all this madness immediately.

Chapter 8

Working It Out

Joi

Beep, beep.

"I'm coming, Joi," Taj yelled.

I knew she wasn't going to be ready. It was 10:45 in the morning, and I had to get there and get back without running into Jaylen.

Beep, beep.

Taj was ridiculous. As she was coming out of her place, I quickly noticed that she was dressed for the club. She did wear her booty shorts, stilettos, and a skimpy blouse. She had taken her braids out, so she did sling on a wig. I knew she had not had a man in a while, but this was way over the top. She was such a pretty girl, but just way too picky. Since she worked at Club Phaze as a manager, you would think that she would be rippin' it with dates. She wanted someone with good hair, whatever that meant. He had to have a six-figure salary, a nice vehicle, and some swagger. You couldn't come at her by talking about diversifying your stock portfolio and purchasing a brownstone in Manhattan. She found these types of men boring. Her ideal man knew how to make her laugh and keep her materialistic butt happy.

"Whew. Sorry about that, Joi. I had to do something with this wig," Taj said when she got in the car.

"Can somebody say 'stripper'?"

"Thanks for the compliment. I try," Taj sarcastically retorted.

"Remind me to buy you a pole for Christmas so you can drop it like it's hot," I teased.

"Did somebody drink some haterade for breakfast this morning?"

"Ha-ha, that was cute, Taj."

As I drove off, I started wondering what I was going to say to Damon. I just wanted all of this to go away so that I could enjoy my life with Jay. I did not want to be looking over my shoulder all the time, either. I finally made it over to the gym. I parked the car across the street just as a precaution. Taj and I got out of my car and started walking toward the front door. But before I reached it, I tripped over my feet.

"Joi, are you okay?"

"Of course I'm okay."

"So what are you going to say to him, Joi?"

"I have no idea. I am at a loss for words. It will come to me when I see him."

I walked up to the counter to ask for Damon.

Taj was too busy checking out the place. It was like being in a candy store.

"Hello. I'm here to speak with Damon," I said.

"Damon who?" asked the male manager at the counter.

"Damon Grant."

"Oh. That's the new guy who played professional football with the Philadelphia Eagles?"

"Yes, I do believe that is him," I replied.

"I have to page him, because I have no idea where he is at the present moment. In the meantime, would you like to take a tour of our new state-of-the-art facility?" asked the manager.

"I would like that very much," Taj interjected, flirting.

"Damon will be up here in a few minutes," the manager assured me.

"Joi, I can stick around for a while and go on the tour later," Taj suggested.

"Girl, please, go on that tour. I will be just fine," I said.

"Okay, but I will be right back," Taj promised.

As Taj walked off with the front-desk manager, I tried my best to relax and stay levelheaded. I started walking toward the window, and I saw Damon walking up in my direction.

"That was fast," I whispered to myself.

"Joi? Was that you who had me paged?" he asked with a slight attitude.

"Yes, Damon. We need to talk," I nervously demanded.

"Go ahead. I'm listening."

"You know, the other day when I ran into you in Philadelphia, it really took me by surprise."

"And why is that, Joi?" He smirked.

"It was just ironic that we bumped into each other. It kinda freaked me out."

"Well, the last time I checked, this is a free country, so we both are free to go where we please."

"So where does it say in this free country that you can grab someone's arm without their consent?" I asked.

"Look, I didn't mean to hurt you. Just say whatever you have to say, because as you can see, I am a very busy man. Now, if you came to tell me that you miss me, then maybe we can work something out."

"That's not what I'm saying, Damon, and you know that. Please stop with all the head games. I am talking about our meeting up in the same place, and you didn't just end up in Old City."

"Oh, I know what this is. You think that I was stalking you or something like that?"

"Look, Damon, I don't want any trouble. I'm married now, and I am sure that you have moved on as well."

"So is that what you came down here to tell me?"

"Well, yeah, because I just don't want any trouble," I said.

"Is that some type of warning? Is that little boy you married going to come after me?"

"Look, I came down here to just talk, but I can see that you are definitely trippin'. Just know this. You fuck with me, and you will wish you was

never born. I'm done. Have a nice fuckin' day!"
I snapped.

"You, too, baby girl. Peace."

"And stop calling me that, you wacko."

After I grabbed my pocketbook, I turned around
to see if I could find Taj. I started to walk around
in the gym, and I spotted her signing up for a
membership. I started feeling anxious, and I just
wanted to leave. Taj was right; he was crazy. Finally,
she got up and headed back toward the lobby.

"Is everything okay?" Taj asked.

I shrugged. "Who knows? I said what I came
down here to say, and that's that. How was your
tour?"

"I joined the gym."

"Wow, that sounds like fun."

"I'm sorry, Joi. Orlando was just so cute. He
took me on a mini tour of the facility and offered
me a bargain that I could not refuse."

"What kind of bargain?" I asked.

"To have dinner with him and he would get me
a lifetime membership for damn near free."

"So what does he get out of the deal?"

"Do you really have to ask, girlfriend? Please."
Taj retorted.

"Please what?" I asked.

"I mean, you are just so uptight. I hate to see
you like this. Let's get everybody together and go
do something fun. Are you down?" Taj asked.

As much as I wanted to say no, I did miss my
girls. We always had a good time together when
we went out. I could use a drink or two.

I nodded. "That sounds good. I'm in. By the way, where has Eboni been hiding?"

"Oh, I forgot to mention that she is in Los Angeles, developing a new artist for her father's record company," Taj replied.

"When did this happen?"

"She left about a week ago. That's why we both were trying to call you."

"So who is the artist?" I asked.

"I am not quite sure, but from what she told me, it's a big deal. He was an independent artist who had been rapping underground for several years."

"Does that mean that he is an old rapper?"

"What's old?" Taj asked.

"Anybody over twenty-five."

"That may be true in some cases, but there are a lot of rappers older than twenty-five, and they puts it down," Taj insisted.

"How old is Jay-Z?"

"Over thirty-five and he is still going and going and going."

"Point well taken, and he is one of the best of all time. Remember he said that thirty is the new twenty?"

"I knew you would see my point when I finished breakin' it down for you. So in the future don't be so quick to judge."

"Okay, Taj. I heard you."

"I'm glad. I just wish I could have seen him and Mary J. in concert over the Christmas holidays down in Atlantic City."

"I'm sure you will get to see him sometime soon because they always seem to be in concert."

"Well, hopefully, when Eboni returns to the East Coast, she will have a lot of hookups. I would love some backstage passes," Taj said.

"Wow. That's a thought because I would love to go see Maxwell," I said.

As I started to drive out of the parking lot, I saw this woman slowly driving past me to park her vehicle. As our eyes met, it was obvious that we had met before, because it was Toni.

"Taj, did you see Toni in that car?"

"Hell, yeah. What is she doing here?" Taj asked.

"I hope she does not go to this gym. I just can't handle Toni and Damon," I grumbled.

"I can call Orlando and find out if she works out there."

"Can you please? I would turn this car around, but I don't want her to notice," I said.

"He gave me his business card. I can call him right now."

"What are you going to ask him? You just can't ask him about Toni. They might be friends or something."

"I'll figure out something. I am coming back tomorrow for my first workout session. Let me see what I can find out."

"Oh, my gosh, Taj, what if Jaylen bumps into Toni at the gym?"

"So what if he does? It's no biggie. That ship has sailed," Taj replied.

"I don't care about that. I just don't want him

at the gym with both Damon and Toni. Who knows what might jump off?"

I needed to call Jordan to see if he could go down to the gym to meet Jaylen. Jordan would make sure nothing happened.

Ring.

"Hello, Jordan."

"What's up, sis? You sound a little stressed."

"Well, I am. You know I have been dealing with some issues involving Damon," I said.

"Yeah, Jay did mention that to me. Are you okay?"

"For now. I am a little concerned about your brother, Jaylen."

"Why? Is he in some kind of trouble?" Jordan quizzed.

"No. It's nothing like that. He is going over to that new gym, Body-Liscious, to confront Damon, and I don't want them two to get into it. On top of that, I think Toni is over there, working out, as we speak."

"Jay's ex Toni?"

"Yes," I said.

"Let me see if I can take an early lunch. I normally go to lunch around one o'clock, but if I can switch with someone, I will leave in a few minutes and hopefully meet him down there. I'll catch a ride."

"I would really appreciate that, Jordan. You are the best brother-in-law in the world."

"I try to be." He laughed.

As I continued to drive, Taj enjoyed the music on her iPod. I just watched her get her party on in the passenger's seat. She removed her earbuds with enough time to conversate briefly before I dropped her off.

"I saw your and Jaylen's wedding picture in the newspaper yesterday. It was fabulous," she remarked.

"Did you say yesterday? Because I searched for it today, and it wasn't in there."

"That's because it was in there yesterday, not today."

"I heard you. The newspaper told me today, so that is the only reason I asked. I didn't think to check yesterday's paper. I can't wait to see it."

"I picked up an extra copy just in case you missed it. It's at my house," said Taj. "Just remind me to get it for you when you drop me off."

"Since we are on the subject, guess whose wedding announcement I did come across today."

"Who?" asked Taj.

"First, you have to promise me that you will not tell a soul."

"I promise."

"Tyree and his girlfriend, Cre'ole."

"Shut the f - - - up! You have got to be kidding me. Does Faith know?"

"Not yet. I have to tell her tonight," I replied.

"That's going to mess her up. She tries to act like she doesn't care anymore, but she does," Taj said.

"I know she does, too, but I know someone who will take Tyree off of her mind, whether or not she is willing to admit it."

"Who?"

"That's not important right now," I said.

"So you'll hook her up, but not me."

"It's Roc. Okay?"

"Roc? Joi, you know I was the first to ask you about him over a year ago."

"I know, but he likes Faith. You can't control who you like."

"That's cool. I'm good."

"You're not mad, are you?" I asked.

"No way José. He's not really my type. I'm a free spirit, and I need somebody who can keep up with me." I drove up to Taj's place and she jumped out of the car.

"Well, Taj, thanks for coming with me down to the gym. Love you!"

"That's how we roll. We are besties for life."

"Bye. I'll call you later."

As I drove off, I realized that I had forgotten to get the extra copy of the newspaper from Taj. I would just check and see if I could pull it up online when I got back to the office. I just did not feel like turning around and going back to Taj's house.

Chapter 9

The Confrontation

Jaylen

I was able to leave the office at 11:30 a.m. so that I could get down to the gym by noon. I called first to make sure that Damon was actually working so I didn't waste my time. There was little to no traffic, so I should be there sooner than I thought.

Ring.

"What's up, little brother?" I said.

"Man, Jay, you're only eight minutes older than me. Mom just saved the best for last." Jordan laughed.

"If you say so. What's good, man?"

"You tell me. I just called to see if you wanted to go and grab a bite to eat."

"Any day but today. I have to take care of something," I replied.

"Something like talking to this Damon character down at the gym?"

"I guess Joi called you."

"Yeah, man. She's just worried."

"I know but it's all good. I'm just going to have a man-to-man. You know. Besides, I don't want you going all out of your way to meet me at the gym."

"I'm already in the neighborhood," said Jordan.

"Where at?"

"In the gym parking lot, so hurry up."

"Jordan, I can handle this dude by myself. Trust me," I argued.

"No doubt. I just want to make sure everything is straight. Anything can jump off."

"Good lookin' out. Just let me do all the talkin'."

"Cool. I can respect that. Hurry up, because I have to get back soon."

It took me ten minutes to get to the gym. I drove into the parking lot and spotted Jordan. We met up with each other. I really didn't want to involve my brother, but it was all good. We'd always been close. He was my identical twin brother, so it was only natural that we should have each other's back. This situation with Joi was getting out of hand. I hated the fact that she was going through this, and it was my duty to fix it. As we approached the lobby area, I asked some dude named Orlando if I could speak with Damon.

"I'll page him for you," said Orlando.

"I'd appreciate that, man."

"Not a problem. Damon Grant to the front

lobby. He is probably with a client. It's been like a revolving door around here. Every time I turn around, somebody is looking for him."

"I bet they are," I replied.

"Yeah, two hot chicks just left here, looking for him, about an hour ago. I guess that's the life of a pro baller. I had to take one of them off of his hands," Orlando bragged.

As Damon approached the lobby, I could see instant frustration on his face. As he got closer, he started to flex his neck and shoulders. At that point I knew we were going to have to have this meeting outside.

"Who's looking for me?" mumbled Damon.

"Damon? I'm Jaylen, and I was wondering if I could speak with you for a minute."

"What's up, man? You must be Joi's husband," said Damon.

"I'm good. Can I talk to you outside?" I said.

"Yeah, whatever, man. Hey, Orlando, I'll be right back. Can you let my client know that I will be back in a few minutes?" Damon said.

Orlando shook his head. "No problem, D."

We went out the front door and walked over to the right side of the building. Jordan stayed close behind Damon.

"So, what can I do for you, partner?" asked Damon.

"Look, man, I don't want any trouble, but my wife has some concerns about you, and as her husband, it's my job to address these concerns," I told him.

"This is some straight-up bullshit, man. Your wife is freaked out because of her own guilty conscience. Believe me, if I wanted to do something to Joi, it would have already been done."

"Look, Damon, I just want to be real clear. Stay away from my wife. If you see her out and about, keep it moving. You have nothing to say to her, and she has nothing to say to you. Are we clear?"

"First of all, I am at work, and I don't want no trouble," Damon growled. "Some shit went down between me and Joi over a year ago, but I'm good. If you want me to stay away from your wife, tell her to stay the f - - - away from my job, and that goes for you, too."

Jordan stepped closer. "What the hell did he say, Jay? He obviously doesn't know who he is dealing with. Don't let this suit fool your ass."

"Jordan, I got this. You see, Damon, you might think you're slick, but I'm going to tell you one thing. If you mess with my wife, I'll kill you. Trust and believe that shit," I assured him.

Jordon pushed me back to prevent a physical confrontation. Damon and I both gave each other piercing stares as he turned and walked back into the gym. The confrontation had drawn a crowd of people from the gym to the door. I got myself together, and no sooner than I did, I looked up and there was my ex Toni walking out the front door.

"Jaylen? What's going on? Are you all right?" she asked.

"He's fine, Toni," Jordan interjected.

"Hi, Jordan. It is so good to see you. Give me some love. I mean, just because your brother and I are no longer married, we still cool. Right?" said Toni.

"Yeah. We cool," said Jordan.

"I must say that you're looking good, Jaylen. So what was that all about? It looked like you two were about to go to blows," Toni remarked.

"It's none of your concern, Toni," I said.

"If you say so. First I see Joi leaving, and now you. Who's next?" Toni replied.

"When was Joi here?" I asked.

"She left about an hour ago. I saw her exiting the parking lot with one of her cronies," said Toni.

"Dammit!" I yelled.

"Did I say something bad?" Toni smirked.

"Toni, not right now," I muttered.

"Well, I really need to talk to you about something. I have been trying to reach you for a while."

"What is it?"

"I'm just going to come right out and ask. I need some money, Jaylen. I know I have no right to ask you, but I am in a financial rut, and there is nobody else I can turn to."

"So why did you come to me? I don't have any money."

"Come on, Jaylen. You got all that money from Miss Daisy. I know you didn't spend it all."

"Wow, I didn't know you had taken a personal interest in my finances, considering we're not married anymore."

"But we were married when she gave you that

money. We were there together on that cruise," Toni reminded me.

"And so were you and K.J., or whatever the hell his name is."

"C'mon, I am desperate. I am having problems paying my mortgage, and it is even harder taking care of a small child. I got laid off from my job a couple of months ago, and now I am collecting unemployment."

"Toni, you graduated from Spelman. You just need to get back on your hustle and grind like everybody else."

"Are you hiring? I'll do anything."

"Wait. Stop it right there. No, I am not, and even if I was, you could not work for me."

"So you're not going to help me?" Toni said.

"Not that I would want any harm to come to your baby, because believe me, I would not wish that on anyone, but as for your mortgage, that's your problem. I told you that it was too much house, but you did what you wanted to do."

"Jaylen, I know, but how was I to know that I would get laid off?"

"And that's my problem?" I retorted.

"Please help me. I only need ten thousand dollars. I will pay you back every dime. I promise," Toni cried.

"Toni, I can't. I'm sorry."

Jordan and I quickly walked to the car and sped away. I must have been doing seventy-five miles per hour. I didn't say a word for five minutes. I wanted so bad to beat the shit out of Damon. Toni was just the icing on the cake, but she had proved to be just who I thought she was, a gold digger. How in the hell was she going to be begging me for money, and she was at the gym? As much as I was angry that Joi had neglected to tell me that she had gone to see Damon, I wasn't going to hold it against her. However, we were definitely going to talk about it when I got home tonight.

"Yo, man, that was some crazy shit that just went down," Jordan said.

"Dude almost got knocked the hell out."

"When I saw how close you got up in his face, I just knew something was about to go down. He was just trying to yank your chain."

"Well, thanks for coming with me. I would probably be in jail right now if you hadn't."

"Hurry up, man. I have to be back to work in seven minutes," Jordan playfully demanded.

I dropped Jordan back off at work. I stopped by my office for a few minutes to grab some files. I had my assistant cancel my appointments for the rest of the day. I would have her reschedule them at a later date. Right now I needed to bring it down. I could only imagine what Joi was dealing with, because in just the short amount of time I spent with Damon, he took me there. I was seeing blood. I knew that my wife was a strong person, but right now she was real fragile. In all the years that I had known her, she could handle just about anything. If a train was coming at her, she could stop it dead in its track. She was no joke. Right now she needed her family. I was going to ask her family to stop by this evening. I'd pick up some takeout from her favorite restaurant so she didn't have to worry about coming home to cook.

"Hey, Mary?"

"Yes, Mr. Payne?" I said on my way out of the office.

"I'm leaving now. Don't forget to cancel my appointments. I will see you early in the morning."

"Okay. Have a good evening."

As I approached my vehicle, it looked like I had a flat tire. When I got closer, it appeared that someone had slashed all four of my tires.

"Damn!" I shouted.

I went back inside my office to call a towing service. They informed me that they would arrive at my location within the hour. I called Joi to let her know that I would be a little late, but I got her machine. I needed to make some calls about the bid I had put in for that project in downtown Philadelphia. I really needed that project because things were getting tight around here. If business continued to be this slow, we wouldn't survive past a year. On the other hand, if they did accept my bid, I would be set for life.

Let me call Faith to see if she can go over to the house and keep Joi company until I get there, I thought.

"Hello, Faith. This is Jaylen."

"Hi, Jay. What's up?"

"Are you busy?"

"A little busy. Why? Does it have to do with Joi?"

"Well, yeah. Someone slashed all four of my

tires, and I need you to go to my house and keep her company for about an hour."

"Sure. I can do that, but I can't leave for at least twenty minutes."

"I understand. Thanks."

"You're welcome."

Chapter 10

Crazy Is as Crazy Does

Faith

I was starting to get the hang of this. I actually loved my job, and my relationship with Miss Delores was getting better and better. I had not been working with her that long, but she was warming up to me quickly. She was like my little granny; only, she was not. I got to see her on a regular basis. I mean, we had our challenges, but I knew that she had a good heart. I couldn't wait to see her little feisty self today. The last time she was here, she wanted me to paint her nails. I was going to give her a pedicure and a manicure. I wanted to do something to her hair, but she wouldn't let anybody touch it. I just wanted to give her a little makeover, because she would look so much better, and I was sure she would feel much better, also. In the meantime, I was going to take a fifteen-minute break and read the newspaper. Joi had said that her and Jaylen's wedding announcement was in there the other day. I'd been so busy that I didn't even get a chance to read it. As I started to thumb through the wedding section, I instantly recognized a photo of Tyree and Cre'ole. For an instant, I felt light-headed. I could not believe what I was seeing.

"That motherfreakin' liar!" I yelled.

"Are you okay, Faith?" Francis frantically asked.

"Yeah, I just saw something that pissed me off, but I really don't want to talk about it."

"That's fine, Faith, but if you need me, I'm here. By the way, Miss Delores is here. Do you want me to take over for you?"

"No, that's okay. I just need a minute to get myself together."

"Faith, you're crying. Are you sure there's nothing I can do?" Francis said.

"I just need some tissue and a few minutes to myself. After that, I'm good."

"Okay. Your wish is my command."

Francis came back with a box of tissues and a glass of water. She left the room to give me my space. This shit had really caught me off guard. I knew I had to get myself together, because I wanted to give Miss Delores a pedicure and manicure today.

Knock, knock.

"Just a minute," I called. *Sniff.*

"Are you all right, dear? Can I get you a drink?" asked Miss Delores as she entered the room.

"No thank you. I have some water."

"What happened that got you so upset? I bet you it's some no-good you know what. I'll kick his ass real good for messin' with my little girl."

I had to laugh because Miss Delores was serious as a heart attack. She went on and on about what she used to do to people who wronged her back in the day. I just blew my nose, and then I washed my hands as she told her story.

"Whoever he is, he does not deserve you," Miss Delores whispered to me.

"Well, we're not together anymore, but I really did love him."

"Did you love him, or was it just lust?"

"I think it was a little of both, but I never slept with him. I wanted to sleep with him, but I broke it off because he had lied to me. I met him over the telephone, when I dialed a wrong number. Afterward, we started talking on the telephone and making plans to meet up. I met him in the Home Depot parking lot. We left and went to a restaurant and ate. We kissed and kissed. It was so romantic. Soon after, I started noticing changes in him. He told me that he lived by himself, but his girlfriend would call from the home number. He didn't know that I knew. I just used to take notice and peek over at his cell. I asked him if he had a girlfriend, and he lied. He had me waiting up for him all night because he told me that he was taking me out. The final straw was when he told me that he had to take his mother some-where, and he showed up at an open mic with his girlfriend-turned-wife while I was reciting my poem. It was crazy. Now I see his wedding announcement in the local paper. I thought I had moved on, but I guess I never really did."

"That was juicy, but good riddance," Miss Delores declared.

"Enough about me. I would like to give you a manicure and pedicure today after your checkup."

"You would do that for me after all the hard times I gave you?"

"Oh, you weren't too bad. Besides, you were just trying to test me," I said.

"Well, you passed the test, because now I look forward to coming here every week. Lord knows, all I do is sit up in that house all by myself, but that's about to change."

"Why do you say that? Is your boyfriend moving in with you?" I playfully asked.

"Oh no. Miss Delores is too old to get her freak on, but back in my heyday, watch out now. I was the J Lu of the sixties. I mean J.Lo. I know you might not believe me, but I was quite the fox. I could have just about any man I wanted, but the one I wanted left me high and dry. He almost took me out."

"Whatchu mean, almost took you out?" I asked.

"I mean, this man was so fine. He was always dressed to kill and could burn up the dance floor. When I was fifteen years old, I would sneak out of the house if I knew he was going to be at the juke joint. The women would line up just to dance with Fast Feet Freddy. He could dance, and boy, could he make love."

"Whoa, Miss Delores. That is way too much information. I don't want to think of you doing it."

"Chile, please! That is just a part of life. All I have is memories. My breasts are hanging with my kneecaps, and every other part is saggin' on me. Ain't no man gonna want me now." She chuckled.

"What happened to him?"

"Vietnam happened to him. One night at the juke joint he told me that he had been drafted and that he had to leave in the morning. I was devastated. He stayed with me all night, lying under a tree. We started planning our future together, and he asked me to marry him. That beautiful night turned into a horrible morning."

"Did you get to say good-bye?" I asked.

"Well, yes. We kissed each other good-bye, and he gave me his address to write. Afterward, I watched his train take off, and I just waved at him until he was no longer in sight. I wrote to him for over a year, but I'm not sure if he ever received any of my letters. There was just so much he needed to know."

"Don't tell me you were pregnant?"

Miss Delores nodded. "Yes, I was. I had a baby girl in the summer of sixty-eight, and I was only fifteen years old. What did I know about taking care of a baby by myself? I didn't have anybody to help me. My two brothers had moved far away, and we lost contact, so I was really alone. I had no family and just a few friends."

"So what happened to your little girl?" I asked.

"I gave her up for adoption because I couldn't take care of her."

"Do you know where she is now?"

"I wish I did."

Miss Delores told me that after she gave her daughter up for adoption, her life took a change for the worse. She started using drugs and selling her body to make a living. She stayed in one abusive relationship after another. However, in 1972 she met this really nice man, and he never raised his hand up to hit her, like her past boyfriends had. He was thoughtful, kind, and caring. After they dated for over two years, she started using drugs again and going back to her bad habits from before. She did not understand why she went back to using drugs. She said that in order to avoid getting hurt again, she decided to mess things up first. He begged her to get her act together, or he was leaving. She never did, so he left and never looked back. However, at the time he left, she was already three months pregnant. History repeated itself again. She gave birth to Henry D. Grant six months later. Miss Delores vowed that she would never give another child up for adoption, because it was too painful, but she soon found it difficult to take care of her son. Henry's father was never told about him.

"Not to be nosy, but I always hear you talking about your son, Henry, but where is he at?" I asked.

"Oh, he is too busy being famous."

"What does he do?"

"You need to ask him that. He'll be home today. Would you like to meet him?"

"I would like that," I said.

"Do you think you can do something to my hair? I want to look real nice. Plus, he is bringing his girlfriend or just his lady friend home."

I was able to finally get her checked out today. She was in a good mood, which made her easy to deal with. She seemed to be really happy. I painted her nails and her feet her favorite color. I washed her hair, then pulled it back into a bun. She whipped out her lipstick and put some on, and girlfriend was looking fierce.

"Go 'head, Miss Delores, with your bad self," I remarked.

"Oh, thank you, Faith. May God bless you, and I will keep on praying for you."

"Wow. You sound so different today."

"I'm just happy to see my Henry. I know you think that I am some crazy old lady, but most of that is an act. I have to keep the money coming, if you know what I mean. My son only paid for the house, and he said that I would have to pay for everything else."

I decided today that I was going to go with transportation to take Miss Delores home. I just had to find Francis to sign off on the paperwork.

"Hi, Francis. Would it be okay if I rode with transportation to take Miss Delores home?"

"Not a problem. I will sign those right now," replied Francis.

Miss Delores and I then patiently waited for

transportation to arrive. We were on our way twenty minutes later. It took about twenty-five minutes for us to get to her house, which was located in Lumberton. As we drove up to the house, it was breathtaking. The driveway formed a circle in front of the home, and the landscaping was beautiful. Miss Delores had it going on. There had to be a golf course nearby, because I spotted some signs. I couldn't wait to see the rest of the house and to hopefully meet Henry. I also noticed two vehicles parked in front. I knew one was a Mercedes, but I couldn't tell what kind of car the other one was. Transportation had to park on the street in front of the house.

"Oh, Miss Delores, your home is fabulous. I can't wait to see the inside," I said.

"Well, come on in. I can't wait for Henry to see my new hairdo. Whew, my back hurts. I need the doctor to check me out tomorrow."

"Are you okay, Miss Delores?" I asked.

"I'll be fine. Now c'mon."

I was about to exit the van when I happened to see a man and a woman walking out the front door. I knew my eyes weren't playing tricks on me. It was Damon and Toni.

What in the hell? I thought.

I was in a state of shock. Everything was starting to add up. Damon was Miss Delores's son. There was no way in hell that I was going to let him see my ass. I was curious as to why she kept calling him Henry. Miss Delores walked back over to the van and asked me to come in the house again. I couldn't think of something to say quick enough. From what I knew of Damon, he was crazy, and he was stalking my best friend, Joi.

Whew, what am I going to do? If he sees me, then that will definitely be trouble. Plus he is in the company of Toni. Either way Damon plus Toni equals disaster.

"Come on in for a minute," Miss Delores said again.

I lied and told her that we had just got radioed in for an emergency and that I would take a rain check. She didn't care, because her son, Damon— I mean Henry, or whatever the hell his name was—was home and with Toni. Now, this was the ultimate bullshit.

Ring.

"Hello, Roc. This is Faith. I really need to talk to you."

"Can you meet me at the Pub on the circle around five thirty?" he asked.

"I'll be there."

Chapter 11

A Real Trip

Joi

It was Saturday, and I couldn't wait to get to the mall. There was so much stuff that I needed. I had to get some clothes and some shoes. My mother's birthday was on Sunday, and I needed to go and get her a present.

"Jaylen? I'll be back. I'm going to the mall," I announced.

"By yourself?"

"Yes, by myself. I'll be all right. I can't keep letting Damon control my life. I am getting ready to take my life back."

"Babe, I know, but make sure you take the necessary precautions to ensure your safety. Basically, don't let your guard down," Jaylen advised.

"Give me a kiss, babe. I love you and I'll be fine."

"I can get dressed really fast and come with you."

"No, Jaylen. I am fine. Besides, you have to meet up with your clients. Don't worry. I can protect myself."

Jaylen was hell bent on being my protector, but I refused to live like a prisoner. Going to the mall was just what the doctor ordered. I needed some me time. But before I started to self-indulge, I needed to call my girl Eboni back. I was so proud of her. She had finally stepped out of the box and started working with an artist. Her father had encouraged her to work closer with the artists years ago, but she hadn't been ready. Although she had an automatic in with her father's record company, she wanted to do it the old-fashioned way. I had so much respect and admiration for Eboni. I wished I could have seen her before she left.

Ring.

"Hello, Eboni?"

"Yes, this is her. Who's calling?"

"Girl, you know this is Joi."

"Silly. I know who this is. I do have caller ID. Where have you been, and why are you just now calling me?"

"I'm so sorry. You know that I love you. I'm just dealing with the madness."

"What madness, Joi?" Eboni asked.

"I'll fill you in when you get back. Right now you need to focus on your career. I'm just so happy for you, girl. So how is it going?"

"We have so much to talk about. You obviously heard that I am developing a new rap artist out here on the West Coast," said Eboni.

"Yes, I did, and I am so excited for you. What's his name?"

"You'll find out when I get back to the East Coast. I am having an album release party and would love it if you and the rest of the crew could come."

"I still can't believe that you upped and moved to Los Angeles," I said.

"I know. I know, but I will be back real soon."

"Okay, Ms. Music Executive. You know I'll be there."

"Great. I have to go now, but I will call you in a few days."

"Smooches."

Eboni and I hung up the telephone before I could ask her if she had met someone special. I would just have to catch up with her when she returned to New Jersey. I continued down Route 38 en route to the mall. I wished there was another way I could go, because I hated all this congestion. But at the end of the day, it was the quickest way to get to the mall from my house. I had thought about going out to the King of Prussia Mall, but driving on the Schuylkill was even worse. I finally turn into Cherry Hill Mall, and it was crowded, as usual. I was hoping to locate a parking space near Macy's. After driving around in a circle, I was able to park off to the left side of Macy's. I didn't mind, because it wasn't too far from the entrance. My only concern was that I had to park my car between a huge SUV and a minivan. I just wasn't completely comfortable from a visibility standpoint.

"What if Damon followed me out here?" I asked myself.

I decided to wait until some people walked past before I got out of my car. I hurriedly jumped out and walked closely behind them. The mall had recently added a Nordstrom to its collection of stores, but it was at the other end. I definitely planned to stop in, because their clothes and shoes were fierce. I just wished that they weren't so damn expensive. I was determined to find me a new dress and some shoes for Eboni's first industry party. I had never been to one, and I was hoping that it wasn't all thugged the hell out. I knew Jaylen was not going to want to go. I mean, he liked some rap music, but not all that crazy stuff.

As I approached the shoe department in Macy's, it looked like a police raid. It seemed like everyone had the same idea I had when I woke up this morning. I started in the shoe department and ended up on the second floor, in the suit department. Eventually, I ended up walking out with two pairs of shoes and a navy blue pin-striped suit. However, I still needed a fly-ass dress, and all I kept seeing was freakum dresses. I could actually hear Beyoncé's song playing in my head. Now that I was married, I had to make sure some of the things I wore looked appropriate. Not that my clothes were inappropriate. You just thought differently about the way you dressed and acted in public. If I could not find one, then I might just wear the same dress I wore to Jaylen and Toni's wedding. I had worn it only once, so it was not like anybody outside of Taj, Eboni, and Faith would recognize it.

I was just not feeling the idea of walking around the mall with all this stuff in my hand, but on the other hand, I wasn't too thrilled about walking back to my car. I just needed to get over this fear of that psycho and go put this stuff in my trunk. Besides, I was parked close enough to the door, so that was even better. First, I have to stop and sit on a bench in the mall to dig out my car keys, which were lodged all the way down in my pocketbook. I looked around for a minute just to make sure I wasn't being followed before I left. Just as I stood up, I saw this young lady who looked just like Vanessa.

"Vanessa? Is that you?" I called.

"Yes, it is. I'm so bad with names."

"Hi. It's me, Joi Thompson. Wil's sister."

"Oh, hi. It's been so long since I last saw you," Vanessa replied.

"Wow, look at you. Where have you been? You look great."

"Thanks and so do you."

"So what have you been up to? Do you live around here?" I asked. "It's so good to see you. You know, after everything with Wil, we just lost touch."

"Well, I'm married, and I have a son named Marcus. My husband and I recently moved back here from Virginia to be closer to my family," Vanessa explained.

"Congratulations. I can't wait to meet them. We

must keep in touch. Wait until I tell my mother that I saw you. She is going to be so happy."

"Well, here's my cell. Give me a call sometime so we can catch up."

"Okay," I said while smiling.

It was so good to see Vanessa. I didn't think that she would ever recover after Wil was murdered. She had never believed that Kendal and her rough-neck ex-boyfriend were innocent. In her mind, they had both set Wil up. Rumors had circulated that Vanessa had had a nervous breakdown. I was not sure how true that was, but based on every-thing that had happened, it was believable. My parents would call to see how she was holding up, and then, after a while, she just disappeared. Just like that. Before I could take two steps, I saw this young teenage boy approach Vanessa, and I could not help but stare him down.

"Hey, Mom. Can you please think about letting me go to that party tonight?" said the boy.

"Marcus, what did I tell you? Now can you go and find your father so that we can go home?" replied Vanessa.

I could not help but go and introduce myself. As I looked over at Vanessa, she gave me this strange look, and I gave her back a strange look. I was shocked as all hell to see the striking resem-blance of Vanessa's son to my brother, Wil. He looked identical to him. They had the same kind of hair, the same eyes, nose, smile, and height. I looked over at Vanessa, and she looked extremely uncomfortable. I was looking equally confused.

"Hello. My name is Mrs. Payne, and I am a good friend of your mother's," I said to the boy.

"Hello, ma'am. My name is Marcus."

"It is a pleasure meeting you, son," I said as I briefly stared into his eyes.

Marcus nodded. "Same here, ma'am. So, Mom, can I go?"

"Marcus, can you please go and find your father? We will talk about this when we get home," said Vanessa.

"Dang, Mom, I am the only sixteen-year-old who can never go hang out with his friends or go to any parties," said Marcus.

Out of nowhere, Vanessa's husband walked up and introduced himself.

"Hi. I'm Robert, and you are?"

"Hi. I'm Joi Payne," I said while extending my hand to shake his.

"The hotshot attorney Joi Payne, who is working on that big murder case?" said Robert.

I shook my head. "Yes, that would be me, but I wouldn't call myself a big hotshot."

"So how do you two know each other?" Robert asked.

"We grew up in the same neighborhood," Vanessa quickly explained.

"Well, it was a pleasure meeting you. Good luck on that case and take care," said Robert.

They started walking out of the mall and Vanessa turned around and signaled me to call her tomorrow. She could tell that I had my suspicions about Marcus. The back of his jersey had TAYLOR on it.

"Marcus Taylor . . . Marcus Taylor. Where do I know that name from?" I said aloud.

It all started hitting me at the same time. Marcus Taylor was that star basketball player that I saw in the newspaper today. Wil was murdered a little over sixteen years ago. This had to be Wil's son. I just didn't remember Vanessa telling us that she was pregnant. Maybe that was the real reason she had just disappeared like thin ice. Vanessa had always insisted that Kendal had started everything because she was upset that Wil and Vanessa were getting back together. So that meant that Wil had definitely been seeing Vanessa around the time of his murder, so that had to be my nephew. I bet that lowlife Kendal had found out about the baby and concocted a story, which led to my brother's murder. Not to mention, Marcus looked nothing like Vanessa's husband, Robert.

"Vanessa? Vanessa? Please wait up," I called.

"Honey, you and Marcus go ahead to the car. I'm right behind you," said Vanessa.

"Vanessa, please! I just need five minutes of your time," I said.

"Yes, Joi."

"Vanessa, it all adds up. Marcus is the spit and image of Wil. That's his son. Isn't it? Please don't lie to me."

"Joi, I can't get into this right now. Can we talk

about this tomorrow? I have to go now. I promise to answer all your questions when you call me."

"Why, Vanessa? All this time you had to know what it would mean to me and my family to have a piece of Wil in our lives. Do you have any idea what this means? Do you? Vanessa, I know that is Wil's son. That's why you're not denying it. He has every right to know about his real father. Wil didn't abandon him. He is his father's legacy, and we have a right to get to know him, too. Oh, my God. What did our family ever do to hurt you? We were there for you, too, when everything happened," I said while sobbing.

"Joi, please calm down. I have to go before my husband gets suspicious. Do you have any free time this week? I would like to meet up with you in private."

"Sure, just tell me the time and place, and I will be there."

"Meet me at the Bonefish Grill on Route Seventy-three in Marlton this Friday at five thirty. Do you know where it is?"

"Yes, I do, Vanessa. So is Marcus coming with you?" I asked.

"No, I am afraid not. At least not this trip. He has a busy schedule with basketball and everything else with school," Vanessa tried to explain.

"Oh, he has a game? Is it local?"

"Joi, I know you have a lot of questions, and believe me, I have all your answers, but just meet me first please."

"Okay. Please accept my apology. I don't mean to be jumpy."

"See you then. Bye. We'll talk. I promise," she begged.

I was so upset, but I did manage to remember the license plate just in case I needed to get her address in the event that she did not call. That whole experience just wiped me out. I could not contain myself. I just broke down. It was like seeing my brother the way I remembered him. It seemed like all my memories of Wil started to bum-rush me all at the same time. Wil had been the best big brother in the whole entire world. We had had such a great relationship. I just wished that he had never met Kendal while he was away at college. I remembered that dreadful telephone call like it was yesterday. It was horrible. Wil was murdered by Kendal's ex-boyfriend, or so Kendal claimed. She lied and created a confrontation between Wil and her lowlife ex named Mack. They got into a fight, and Wil was shot to death by Mack. To make matters worse, Mack claimed self-defense and got off scot-free.

My shopping trip was a wrap. I was just going to have to come back tomorrow to get the rest of the stuff. Once everyone knew that Marcus Taylor was Wil's son, it would bring so much happiness and closure to our family. I just knew my brother had sent us down an angel, and his name was Marcus.

Chapter 12

Damon Strikes Again

Joi

After I put my stuff in the car, I realized that I really needed to run back inside and quickly grab a gift card for my mother's birthday. I was already amped after seeing Vanessa and Marcus.

What could top that? I thought.

No sooner than I closed the trunk to my car, I felt the presence of someone behind me.

"Funny meeting you here," said a male voice.

"Funny, my ass," I growled.

"It's a free country. Who said I wasn't allowed at the Cherry Hill Mall?"

"Damon! What the fuck are you really doing here?" I yelled.

"I love it when you get mad, baby girl."

"I'm calling the police."

"Listen here, bitch! You think that you can go around and mess up my life. I lost my job and my home because of you. I should choke your little ass right now, you slimy-ass snitch."

"Damon, I am going to tell you one more time to get the hell away from me. You seem to have forgotten that I am an officer of the law."

"Whoop-de-fuckin'-do. Now I suggest that you open that car door, get in, and do as I tell you. Shit, I might as well hit it one more time."

Roc and some other dude came out of nowhere. Roc grabbed Damon and put him in a choke hold from behind. Damon tried to wrestle his way out of the hold, but Roc had him.

"Man, stay the f- - - away from her!" Roc yelled at Damon.

"This ain't got nothin' to do with you," Damon muttered.

"Yo! Rick, man, call the police, because I might kill this dude," said Roc.

"Look, man, let me go, a'ight? I wasn't going to hurt her. I just want to talk to her for a minute," Damon mumbled.

"Man, you don't have nothing to talk to her about. Man, you need help," Roc thundered.

"Roc, let him go," I said.

Roc frowned. "Are you sure?"

"Not really, but that's my decision for right now," I replied.

"Are you absolutely sure, Joi?" Roc asked.

I nodded. "Yeah, I just want him to leave me the hell alone."

Roc let Damon go and pushed him forward so that he could walk away. For some reason, I wasn't trippin' like I normally was. I needed to stand up to him. I knew Jaylen was not going to be happy with my decision, but I needed to regain control of my life.

"How did you know that I was here?" I asked.

"Trust me. I just did." Roc smiled. "Are you okay to drive home, Joi?"

"Yes, I am. Thanks for coming to my rescue, but I have to figure this out on my own. I can't let him win." I just hoped that I had made the right decision.

"I still think that you should go down to the police station and report him."

"I am definitely going to do that. He can run off, but he can't hide."

"Call me when you get home," said Roc.

"I will. How in the world did I ever get mixed up with someone like him?"

While all of this was going on with me at the mall, Jaylen was dealing with his own drama. He had received a call while I was gone from his bank, saying that some woman posing as his wife was trying to cash a check for fifty thousand dollars. Jaylen soon discovered that the woman in question was Toni. Wachovia had given her a blank check, and she had made it payable to herself and had signed Jaylen's name. Luckily, someone from the bank had recognized Toni and called Jaylen. They showed him the surveillance tape, and there she was, big as day. The bank put a fraud alert on his account and contacted the police. Jaylen filed a police report on Toni for fraud.

Later over dinner at home, I filled Jaylen in on what happened with Damon at the mall. We both went to the police station to finally file restraining orders on both Toni and Damon.

"That was the shopping trip from hell, and I still didn't get my mother's birthday present." I chuckled.

"How can you find it in you to laugh at a time like this? I know I don't feel like laughing," replied Jaylen.

"You know, Jay, when Damon got all up in my face, I was scared and pissed all at the same time. I just held my ground, and it felt good because it was the old me. I miss that."

"So your superwoman instincts kicked in?"

"Hell yeah, they did. I truly believe that I would have hurt him. Hmmm. I like the sound of that, too. From this point on, let's not say his name anymore. For now on, his name is *it*."

"I can't argue with that or *it*."

"So what should we call that bitch Toni?" I asked.

"Uh, how 'bout *nobody?* So when I tell you that I bumped into *nobody,* you'll just know."

"Works for me, but if *nobody* tries to write another check, somebody is going to whip her ass."

"*Nobody* is really going to be up shit's creek when she has to go to court for trying to write a fraudulent check."

"So in other words, somebody named *nobody* may have to do some time, and *it* might get a beat down?" I jokingly asked.

"I tell you what. Why don't I go slip into something comfortable and we just enjoy each other's company and forget about *it*, because they are *nobody* to us? You grab the wineglasses and turn on some Maxwell, and I will be back in a few."

"You're good."

An hour later.

Ring.

"Hello, Joi. This is Pop. Jordan's been in an accident, and Jaylen needs to get down to the hospital."

"What happened? Oh, my gosh, Pop, is it serious?" I cried.

"Put Jaylen on the telephone please," he said, sounding upset.

"Hi, Pop. What happened to Jordan?" Jaylen asked.

"All I know is that he was in an accident in your car, and he is hurt pretty bad. I don't know if he is going to make it."

"I'm on my way," said Jaylen.

"Jaylen! What in the hell is going on around here? Why is all this shit happening to us? I can't take it anymore," I cried.

"Joi, calm down. I need to drop you off at your parents' so that I can get up to the hospital."

"No, I have to be there."

"Joi, listen to me. Jordan is going to be just fine. I need you to go and get some rest. I will call you as soon as I hear something. I need to know that you are safe so that I can focus on Jordan. You being at your parents' home will let me know that you are."

Jaylen dropped me off at my parents' house, and then he went to the hospital to check on his twin brother. My mother made me some hot tea to help me relax.

"Mom, let me know as soon as Jaylen calls. Please," I said.

"I will, sweetheart."

I laid down on the sofa and slept for what seemed to be an eternity, Jaylen called my parents' home around 12:30 a.m., and I answered the telephone.

"Hi, Jaylen. What are the doctors saying?"

"Well, Jordan lost a lot of blood, so I had to donate some. There are some internal injuries, but they are not sure of the extent. They may have to do surgery, but the doctor said he would let us know. I sure hope not. He is critical but stable for now. He's not breathing on his own, and there is some trauma to his head."

"What happened?" I asked.

"I spoke to the police officer, and he said that Jordan lost control of the car, and it flipped over three times in the street. The only thing that saved him was his seat belt, which he barely wears."

"Thank you, Jesus."

"My parents are with him right now. The doctor asked us to limit the number of visitors at one time. The police are investigating the accident, and the vehicle was sent to their repair shop to make sure nothing was deliberately done to cause an accident."

"Well, if you need to stay up there, I do understand. I'll stay here until you come and pick me up," I said.

The next morning.

Ring.

"Hi, baby. How is Jordan doing?" I asked.

"He's still fighting. He had a rough night, but the doctor said he needs to get through the first forty-eight hours. The police called me first thing and said that someone deliberately cut the brake wires, so that is most likely how Jordan lost control. First, somebody slashes my tires, and now this. Whoever did this is after me, not Jordan. Now my brother is in there fighting for his life, instead of me."

"Jay, let's not focus on that right now. The police will get whoever did this."

"Who did this? I'll tell you who did this. That fuckin' Damon is responsible."

"Jaylen, it could have been anybody. Let's get proof first. If Damon is responsible, believe me, he will pay."

"Well, I might not wait that long, because I got

all the proof I need." A few minutes later, Jaylen and I ended the call.

Ring. It was my cell phone.

"Hey, Faith. What's going on?"

"Joi, I heard about Jordan, and I am so upset, but that's not the only reason why I am calling you."

"What's wrong? You're scaring me."

"Joi, do you remember me telling you about my patient Miss Delores and how I was going with transportation to take her home one day? I told you that she had a son who was famous, and he had purchased this beautiful home for her."

"Yes, Faith. Can you make a long story short?"

"Okay, okay. You'll never guess in a million years who her son is."

"Who, Faith?"

"Are you sitting down?"

"Yes, Faith. I am sitting down," I lied.

"Damon, but she calls him Henry."

"Get the hell outta here. Are you serious?"

"Serious as a heart attack, but that's not it."

"Well, what more could there be?" I asked.

"He wasn't alone."

"So, what do I care if he wasn't alone?"

"Oh, you would most definitely care about this," Faith said.

"Who was he with?"

"Toni. Before you even ask, yes, Toni, Jaylen's ex."

"I should have put two and two together when I saw her at the gym where Damon works."

"Well, I had to tell you, because those two to-

gether spell disaster. I am meeting up with Roc
at five thirty."

"I gotta go," I said.

Immediately after I hung up the telephone, I
was enraged. Now my suspicions were confirmed.

That was why everything around us was crum-
bling. I had been so focused on Damon that I'd
lost sight of the big picture. Now Jaylen and I had
two nuts on the loose, but now they had messed
with the wrong person. It was about to be on.

I went home to take a quick nap. I had been tired
for weeks now from the wedding and working.
I needed to get up to the hospital to see Jordan. I
poured myself two glasses of merlot to take the edge
off. Before I knew it, I had passed out.

*"Don't move, baby girl. I'm not going to hurt you. I
promise that I will be gentle."*

*"Ahhh, don't do this. Ouch! You're hurting me.
Please somebody help me. I can't see," I complained.*

"Just cooperate and I won't hurt you, like I said."

*"Please don't do this. You are being too rough. Get off
of me," I sobbed.*

*"Shut the fuck up! I will get off of you when I'm
done. Now turn over so I can hit it from the back."*

*"I can't. Why are you doing this to me? I just want
to get some sleep."*

*"Hey, help me turn this bitch over. She's not going to
see you. Her ass is drugged up. I couldn't wait for her
to drink that damn wine." He laughed.*

*"Oh, my gosh, oh, my gosh, you're hurting me. I can't
take it," I cried faintly.*

"Why are you pounding on her like that? You said we

would only be here for fifteen minutes, and you're going at it like you're trying to make up for lost time," the female replied.

"Mind your damn business," he responded.

"Why are you raping her?" the female asked.

"Go and wait downstairs until I'm done," he yelled.

"Please, somebody help me," I pleaded.

"I'm just about there. Damn, I miss you. Now I'm done. Big Daddy will tuck you in now."

Two hours later.

"Joi? Wake up, sleepyhead."

"Jaylen? Where were you? I had this really bad dream, and people were talking, but I don't want to talk about it right now. Just hold me."

"Don't worry. I'm here, baby. I got worried when you didn't show up at the hospital and you didn't answer your phone."

"I didn't hear the phone. I drank two glasses of wine and lay down. I had every intention of getting up in about an hour, but I overslept."

As I went to get up, my body was hurting all over and my legs were trembling. Another strange thing was that my vagina was hurting really bad. It felt like somebody had bit my nipples, and there were scratch marks on my buttocks.

"What the hell happened? Was that a dream I had, or was it real? Jay, were the doors locked when you came in?"

"Of course. Why do you ask?"

"No reason."

I slowly walked into the bathroom and took a shower. Maybe something was in my wine. I was not sure what had happened, but something had happened. I felt like I had been raped, but by whom and how? I silently cried in the shower. I couldn't go to the police with a story like this. How would I sound? "Um, I think I was raped tonight. I can't remember everything, because I had two glasses of wine."

"What if Damon broke into our home and raped me while Jaylen was up at the hospital? I have to tell Jaylen. No, I can't. Not until I am sure."

I remembered that something had been over my face and I couldn't see. I was going to have to figure this one out before I could decide what to do. I went back to the bedroom and started changing the linen. As a matter of fact, I was going to throw this entire set out. I looked down at the sheets to see if there was anything that could link Damon, or anybody else for that matter, to a possible rape. While thoroughly checking the sheets, I spotted some possible evidence. Bingo.

Chapter 13

Mistaken Identity

Damon

Ring.

"Hello?"

"Toni, where is your dumb ass at?"

"Don't start, Damon. I have a life, too."

"Where the f - - - are you, Toni?"

"I just left Kenyatta. He won't let me see our son. I am just so sick and tired of dealing with him. I can't wait to go to court to get full custody of him."

"Well, as long as your broke ass is living under my roof, you need to make sure you're available when I call."

I needed to figure out how I was going to get to Joi and Jaylen without fucking everything up. This shit was throwing a monkey wrench in my plans.

"There ain't no way I'm going to let the little

happy couple ruin me," I muttered. "I would love to kill that punk-ass n - - - Jaylen, because he thinks that he can just come down to my job and disrespect me."

"Is that all you can think about? I mean, I want revenge on that prissy behind Joi, but my son is more important right now," Toni snapped.

"Where I'm from, respect is everything. That bitch is going to regret the day she ever screwed me over."

"Whatever, Damon. I see that what I am saying means nothing. I'll see you in about an hour."

"Where are you going?" I asked.

"I have to stop by the gym and pick something up."

If only I could get stupid-ass Toni to do what I wanted and figure out a way to set her up to take the fall. I definitely didn't want her staying at my mom's crib longer than she had to. The bottom line was that she had to go. To this day, I still couldn't figure out how I coincidentally bumped into Jaylen's ex at the wedding. I thought I was incognito, and here she was, dressed in disguise. After seeing that private investigator Roc, I knew I had to jet. As soon as I stepped out of the church, I literally ran smack-dab into this woman. I had to help her keep her balance, because the impact almost knocked her over. Out of nowhere, she recognized me from television. This female knew my name, what team I played for, my relationship with Joi. I pulled her across the street to see what else she knew. The last thing I was trying to do was get caught. After she recognized me, I just figured that someone else might have also recognized me.

After a brief conversation, it was obvious that we were both there for the same reason. Toni claimed that Joi had disrespected her by coming to her wedding, so she just figured that she would return the favor. At one point, she just pulled off her wig and admitted to not caring if anybody saw her. I had personally known that it was over between Joi and me, because she was in love with this Jaylen character, who I despised for my own selfish reasons. I had started trippin' because rejection wasn't an option for me, and that made me want her even more. She had made me feel like I had nothing to offer anybody. Her actions toward me had increased my insecurities, which had made everything else in my life spiral downward. This bitch had exposed my weaknesses and so much other shit I was dealing with.

I never had a relationship with my father, and my mother was mentally strung out. I was told that I had an older sister, who had been adopted, and two uncles who lived on the West Coast, but what good was that if they weren't around? I definitely had issues that made me do some crazy shit. After I went to college on a football scholarship, I started using my middle name as my first. I hated the name Henry. It sounded like an old man's name. I'd been a fucked-up individual then, and I still was, but I hadn't wanted Joi to know it. Yet she'd seen right through me. In a strange way, I felt like if she would only accept me, then everything else would fall into place. However, right now there was no turning back for me. I'd lost my job, my home, my self-respect, and most of all, my girl. Joi had betrayed me by turning me in and then marrying somebody else. Bottom line, if I couldn't have her, nobody else would. Besides, she was the only woman who satisfied my sexual appetite, even when she was sleeping.

Ring.

"Hey, Juan. This is Damon. Yo, man, did you cover all your tracks with that car?"

"I did exactly what you asked me to do. If anybody survives through this, they must have nine lives."

"You definitely got the right car?"

"Yo, man, chill out. I checked everything out. The car was registered to Jaylen Payne, and it was in the shop, getting the tires repaired."

"I just want to make sure that my hands are clean. Shit, I'm in enough trouble. I'm just trying to keep the man off my back," I said.

"Yo, man, I did exactly what you asked me to do," Juan said.

"Cool. I'll get with you later at the club," I said, with a great big grin on my face. After I hung up the phone with Juan, I looked down at my phone and saw that Toni was calling me.

Ring.

"Hello, Damon. This is Toni. What the fuck were you thinking?"

"What's your problem?"

"I thought you were only trying to scare them? I just read in the paper that Jordan Payne is in critical condition and fighting for his life."

"Jordan? I thought it was Jaylen," I grumbled.

"Well, you thought wrong. The newspaper also said that there was proof of the vehicle being sabotaged. Apparently, somebody cut the wires to the brakes on Jaylen's car."

"Whatchu so upset for?"

"That's a stupid question to ask, Damon. First of all, Jordan is my friend. He is the only one in the family who ever accepted me when I was married to Jaylen. If I knew that he would get hurt, I would not have agreed to help you."

"How in the hell was I supposed to know his brother was driving his car?"

"That's not for me to figure out. You're the one calling all the shots," Toni snapped.

"Girl, shut up. Ain't nobody gonna find out nothing, because there is nothing to find out."

"You know I'm fighting for custody of my son. What if Jordan dies, Damon? I need to be there for my son. I can't lose my son, Damon. I wish I'd never met you at the wedding. I'm done with this."

"Hey, you approached me at the wedding and introduced yourself to me. Trying to act like you knew this and knew that about me. I went along with you on everything so that my cover would not be blown. Besides, you couldn't have been too concerned, considering you were writing all those fraudulent checks."

"Who cares, Damon? You ain't shit. All you did was use me," Toni muttered.

"Use you? For what? Look at you. You're a college graduate with no job, no money, no nothing."

"Oh, please don't go there. Look at you. You are an ex-football-playing has-been who has moved back with his mother because of his criminal background."

"Well, you'd better not be down there, singing like a bird," I yelled.

Click.

"I know she didn't hang up the telephone on me. Now I am going to have to go and drag her back to the house," I raged.

I took off in my car to go and find Toni. As much as I wanted to knock her the hell out, I couldn't risk it, because she knew too much. My boy Juan had messed up, because he hadn't gotten the right person. Now I was going to have to take matters into my own hands. The only fuckin' thing Juan had done right was to follow Jaylen's and Joi's asses on their honeymoon. I had had him send champagne and roses to their honeymoon villa. My goal was to get Jaylen, and after I got him out of the way, my next move was to get Joi. I wanted that bitch to jump every time she heard my name. I just had to figure out a way to get this private investigator off of my trail. I needed to figure out a way to get rid of him, too. As I pulled up to the gym, I parked my car on the side of the building. I needed to get in and out. As I walked through the door, I saw Toni talking to Orlando.

"What's up, man?" I said.

"I hear that you the man, Damon," Orlando said.

"Toni?" I said.

"What, Damon? I came to work out and clear my head," Toni barked.

"That's cool, but I really need to talk to you in the back for a minute," I replied.

Toni frowned. "Can we talk back at the house? I just want to be left alone."

"Look, I need you to walk in the back office for a minute," I said while grabbing Toni's arm.

I threatened Toni to walk in the back. I could not risk her making any telephone calls or talking to the wrong people in order to save her ass. She reluctantly walked into the back office. There were a few onlookers watching us, but they were probably thinking we were having a lovers' quarrel. After we went in the back, I slammed the door and grabbed Toni's arm again.

"Don't you ever disrespect me again," I yelled.

"Damon, let me go, please. You are hurting my arm."

"I don't like what I was hearing from you on the telephone earlier."

"What are you talking about, Damon? I didn't say anything."

"I'm talking about what happened to your ex-brother-in-law, Jordan, or whatever the fuck his name is."

"I just don't want any parts of it, because if he dies, we're both going down," Toni stated.

"Well, too late for that, but I've covered all my tracks, so what are you worried about?"

"Nothing. I just can't risk losing my son, that's all."

"I can't believe that I am hearing this from a woman who is trying to cash fraudulent checks from her ex-husband's bank account and to hack into strangers' credit cards."

"Well, it's not like I was able to do either one," Toni muttered.

"Look around, Toni. There are cameras everywhere you go. For you to have a degree in computers, you don't have a clue when it comes to hacking."

"Please. I know how to hack into anyone's account, but some of them had some high-tech security codes on their cards. Besides, I wore a disguise. I've done this a million times."

"I still think that was a stupid move," I said.

"Yeah, well, Jaylen wouldn't have me arrested. He'll just find me and start yelling and threatening to have me locked up."

"Believe what you want to believe, but if you decide to go to the police with what you know, you're going to wish that you were locked up."

"Your boy screwed up bad. What if Jordan dies, Damon?"

"Well, I guess you will be going to a funeral," I joked.

Knock, knock.

"Hey, Damon. Everything all right back here?" called Orlando.

"We cool, man. Just having a little disagreement, Orlando," I replied.

"Toni, you all right?" said Orlando.

"Yeah, I'm good," Toni lied.

"Man, I told you that we were all right," I muttered.

"Just doin' my job, Damon," said Orlando.

As soon as Orlando left, I told Toni to leave. Now I had to add her to the list of people I had to watch, because one slipup from her could mess up everything. I waved good-bye to Orlando, and as soon as Toni and I approached the door, a man walked in.

"Are you Damon Grant and Toni Payne?" the man asked.

"Yes, sir, I'm Damon."

"And I'm Toni."

"Here. These are for you. Have a good day," said the man.

"What is it, Damon?" Toni asked.

"Give me a second to open it up," I said. "It's a restraint order from Jaylen and Joi Payne."

"I have the same thing," Toni cried.

"Dammit," I yelled.

"Is everything okay, man?" Orlando asked.

I nodded. "I'm good. C'mon, Toni. Let's go."

Taj

"Orlando? Was that Damon and Toni leaving?"

"Yeah. Why, baby? Where are you going, and what's the matter?"

"I was in the back room, looking for that equipment you asked me to get. Damon and Toni came in screaming and yelling, so I hid behind the other door, and they were talking about my friend Joi, Jaylen, and his brother. Damon tried to kill Jaylen, but apparently Jordan got hurt instead. I have to go to the police."

"Wait up, Taj. I'm going with you," Orlando said.

"You can't just leave the gym. I will call you as soon as I get there."

"You're right. I'm here for you, so don't forget."

I couldn't believe what I had just heard and seen. Thank goodness I'd been able to whip out my cell phone and record a video containing most of it. My hands had been trembling so bad after I figured out what they were talking about.

Joi is going to flip out when I tell her about this, I thought to myself.

I could not wait to call Faith, but I wanted to call Joi first. But I needed to calm down first. I was having heart palpitations and flashes all at the same time.

Chapter 14

Taking Matters Into My Own Hands

Faith

It was 5:15 p.m., and I was sitting here at the Pub waiting for Roc to meet me. Joi was my best friend, and there was way too much going on, and I needed to let Roc know, because he'd know what to do. I wanted to get there a little early because my nerves were jumping all over the place.

I can't believe Damon and Toni know each other and that Damon is Miss Delores's son, I thought to myself.

I kept looking around the parking lot in search of Roc's vehicle. Damon and Toni had to be stopped. What if they were responsible for hurting Jordan? I couldn't even imagine. At 5:27 p.m., I saw Roc pull up. He got out of his vehicle and walked over to mines.

"Faith, what's going on? It sounded urgent."

"Roc, I think Joi and Jaylen are in way over their heads in dealing with this Damon character."

"Why? What else happened?"

I started explaining everything about Miss Delores being Damon's mother and how I found out. Roc was in utter shock. He knew that Damon was into some crazy activities, but finding out about Damon and Toni pushed him into another gear.

"Thanks for letting me know. Your girl Joi had a run-in with Damon at the mall. Luckily, me and my partner Rick walked up on them, because who knows what might have happened."

"Roc, I am scared for Joi. What if Damon had something to do with Jordan's accident? We have to do something quick and fast, because if that bastard tries to hurt Joi, I will kill his ass," I sobbed.

Roc pulled me close to him, pulled out a tissue from his pocket, and wiped my tears. I was not sure what I was experiencing, but from that moment, being in Roc's arms felt safe. He continued to hug me and rub my back.

"Are you all right?" he asked.

"I feel a little better."

Roc lifted my chin, and he looked at me with those dark, piercing eyes and kissed me. My initial reaction was to immediately return the gesture. We kissed for what seemed an eternity. I couldn't believe it. I was actually kissing Roc, and it just felt so right. Afterward, he just stood there and stared at me for a few moments.

"I hope I wasn't out of line," he said.

"I didn't mind. Besides, it just happened naturally between two consenting adults," I said, staring into his eyes.

Roc started to laugh. Out of all the times that I had seen Roc in action, this was the first time that I saw a shy side to him. I thought it was cute. As much as I had Joi on my mind, I needed this time-out. Roc was like a brother to Joi, and I was like her sister. So we automatically had something in common. I was not sure if I was ready to jump back into the dating scene just yet. There was just so much going on, and I still had a lot to learn with my new job.

"You know, Faith, I've always been attracted to you," he confessed.

"That's interesting to know." I smiled.

"Well, if you are not busy sometime, I would like to take you to dinner."

"I would like that, Roc," I said, smiling.

"I would like that, too," he said while returning the smile.

After sharing a brief moment of reintroduction, we jumped back into friendship mode.

"So, what's next with everything that is going on? How can I help?" I asked.

"Don't worry. I've been working behind the scenes in regards to Damon. I am waiting for some documents on this dude to come over to my office."

"Documents? Like what?" I asked.

"Stuff like where he's from, his family. You know, personal stuff."

"Well, now that you know who his mother is, that should be of some help."

"Yeah, that's going to be a big help."

"Well, we need to get on it right away. I'm available the rest of the evening," I said.

"Well, love, I mean Faith, I have to go and meet up with Rick. Can I call you later?"

"Sure. Do you have my number?"

"I'm sure I can retrieve it somehow. I mean, you just called me, and a number did pop up." He chuckled.

"Oh yeah, I forgot that I was talking to a private investigator. Let me give you an alternate number to reach me at in the event you retrieve some additional information."

He took my number and reached down and kissed my cheek. "I'll call you later," he said.

Wow. I didn't know what to do with myself. I did not think that I would have that type of reaction to Roc, but when he started hugging and comforting me, it just felt so good and so right. Maybe it could be me responding to pure loneliness, especially after dealing with Tyree. It had taken me a minute to realize that he wasn't worth my time. He had had me wasting all my good poetry on his dumb ass. After all that, he had turned around and married the supposedly nutty ex-girlfriend, who had seemed perfectly normal when I met her. I didn't know what I'd been thinking all this time or what the hell I'd been looking for. Now along came Roc. This man had indirectly expressed his interest in me several times to Joi, and I had just kept blowing him off. Again, what had I been thinking? What a fool I had been, but no more. I wanted to get to know him better after all this craziness was over.

Ring.

"Hello?"

"Joi? It's me, Faith. How is Jordan?"

"Well, the last I heard from Jaylen, he was still hanging in there. He is critical but hanging."

"What happened?" I asked.

"I am not exactly sure. All I know is that Jordan picked up Jaylen's car from the shop, and he lost control and had an accident."

"Was he drinking or something?"

"No, he was not. However, Jaylen seems to think that Damon had something to do with it," Joi revealed.

"Why? I mean, I am not surprised, but why does Jaylen think that?"

"Well, the police told him that someone had deliberately cut the wires to the brakes. I mean, the reason why the car was in the shop was that someone had recently slashed the tires on it at his job. He thought Toni might have had something to do with the tires because he refused to loan her some money."

"I just cannot believe that you guys are going

through all this so soon after you got married. This is supposed to be a happy time for you both."

"For better or for worse," Joi replied.

"Well, I was so upset about everything that I called Roc."

"Why did you call him? He's already been trying to help me as much as he possibly can. I appreciate everything that he does for me, but I can't rely on Roc all my life. I have to start fighting back. What kind of damn life would I be living? It is time for me to get back on track and not let the situation take control of me. I have to take control of the situation."

"Well, he met me at the Pub, and I told him about Miss Delores. We kissed, and he is going to call me later so that we can figure something out."

"Wait just a freakin' minute. Hold up. I know you did not think that you were going to fast-talk me and slide that tidbit of juicy information past me. Oh no, you didn't," Joi bellowed.

"Didn't what, Joi?"

"Did I hear you say that you and Roc were kissing?"

"Did I say kiss?"

"Yeah, girl. Ooohhh, tell me everything," Joi demanded.

"Come on, Joi. You have enough to worry about. What Roc and I did just happened. We were just two consenting adults caught up in a moment. There's no reason to bog you down with the details."

"Girl, please, the crazy week that I've been having,

I need some good news. My two best friends might be hooking up. I knew it. I just knew it. I am so happy for you two."

"Uh, calm down, Joi. It was only a kiss, not a marriage proposal. Besides, I can't focus on anything else right now."

"Faith, you are like my sister, and I love how protective and supportive you, Roc, and everybody else have been, but I am a grown woman. Jaylen and I got this. I didn't go to law school to let someone just break the law."

"I know you two probably got this situation under control, but now with Jordan being in the hospital, Jaylen has to divide his focus. Damon and Toni are double trouble. So please let us help you."

"You're right. I just don't want anything to happen to you guys, trying to help us," Joi replied.

"Well, I know that if I was in a similar situation, you would be there for me."

"You know that I would."

"Well, let me be there for you," I pleaded.

"So, Faith, what's our next move?"

"The hell if I know," I jokingly said.

Ring.

"Joi, I have to get the other line. It's Taj," I said.

"Okay, Faith. Call me later," Joi replied.

"Hey, Taj. What's up, girl?"

"Hi, Faith. Is Joi with you?"

"No, she is at her parents' home. Why? You sound like something is the matter."

"Girl, I was going to call Joi first, but I changed

my mind because she is dealing with way too much right now. You aren't going to believe what just happened down at the gym. I am on my way down to the police station. Can you meet me there, and I will tell you all about it?"

"Tell me now," I snarled.

"I can't drive and talk on the cell when I am nervous."

"What happened? What are you talking about, Taj?"

"Wait. Let me pull over real quick."

"Okay."

"I was at the gym, and Damon and Toni were arguing about what had happened to Jordan, and about all this other stuff. They didn't know that I was in the back office, getting something behind the door," Taj started explaining ten miles a minute.

"Wait. Hold up, Taj. You need to calm down and speak slower. I can't fully understand what you are saying."

"Okay. I was at the gym, visiting Orlando. He asked me to go in the back to get something for him. No sooner than I walked in, I heard voices close to the office. They had no idea that I was even back there. From what I gathered, both Damon and Toni had something to do with what happened to Jordan. I don't know how deep Toni is involved, but she is somehow. She said something about not wanting to lose her son if Jordan dies."

"Oh, my gosh, Taj, are you freakin' serious?" I asked.

"As a heart attack."

"I will call Joi and tell her. This is just something she is going to have to suck up and handle. I am on my way."

Chapter 15

Keeping the Faith

Joi

I hung up the telephone with Faith, but she called right back ten minutes later. She filled me in on everything Taj had told her. I actually had to take a minute to get myself together. Faith said that she and Taj were on their way to the police station. I told Faith that I was on my way to meet them there. I slammed the door at my parents' house and immediately hopped into my car.

"Joi! Where are you speeding off to?" Mom yelled, standing between the doors.

"Oh, don't worry. I will be back in about an hour. I have to meet Faith and Taj downtown."

"All right now."

I did not want to start driving downtown like a maniac, nor did I want to worry my mother. I had completely underestimated both Damon and Toni. They had to be held accountable for their actions. I mean, they had almost killed Jordan, and if he died, they were going to be charged with murder. Wow, I had so much going through my mind right now. I still had to deal with my situation. If I had been raped, and I was sure that I had been, I needed to get to the bottom of this. All of this seemed so surreal. Things were starting to add up, but the final answer was still a mystery. First, I had found out that Damon's mother was a patient at the hospital where Faith worked. Faith went with the transportation department to drop off Miss Delores and saw Damon and Toni together at this woman's house, and she turned out to be his mother. I mean, I knew Damon was crazy, but he spared no expense in trying to get revenge on me. I mean, bumping into him down in Old City was too much of a coincidence, but it must be a part of his plan in his twisted mind. Next, he ended up at Cherry Hill Mall and tried to attack me. That last nightmare had me freaked out.

For the life of me, I still just didn't understand how he and Toni had hooked up. That one was still throwing me for a loop. Now Taj had overheard Damon and Toni arguing at the gym about what happened to Jordan. Damon had flat-out admitted that Jaylen had been his target and not Jordan. This bitch Toni was trying to write bad checks against Jaylen's account. These two were way out of control. But that was okay because they did not have any more time to mess over Jaylen and me. Hopefully, they had already gotten served with the restraining orders.

I'd been so busy that I had not even gotten a chance to call Vanessa back regarding Marcus. After I met Taj and Faith at the police station, I needed to get over to the hospital to talk to Jaylen.

Ring.

"Hello, Jaylen," I said.

"Hey, baby. What's wrong?"

"I need to talk to you, but not right now. I was going to come over to the hospital in about an hour."

"It sounds important," said Jaylen.

"It is important, but it can wait for an hour."

"Joi, please tell me what is wrong right now."

"You were right," I admitted.

"Right about what?"

"About Damon. I just spoke to Faith, and she told me something very disturbing, and it has to do with what happened to Jordan. I really hate talking about this over the telephone."

"What are you talking about, Joi? Just tell me everything."

"Faith said Taj overheard Damon talking to Toni at the gym."

"About?"

"About what happened to Jordan. You were the target, but things did not go as planned. Damon had someone name Juan cut the brake wires on your car. That accident was meant for you. Jordan was just in the wrong place at the wrong time."

"Are you sure, Joi?"

"I am so sure, I am on my way to meet Taj and

Faith downtown right now so that Taj can give a statement to the police."

"I knew I should have picked up my own car. This is all my fault," Jaylen moaned.

"Jaylen, please don't say that. You would have done the same thing for him."

"Damn, I want to go with you, but Jordan is about to go into surgery and I . . ."

"Jay, it's okay. That is your brother, and you are where you need to be. I got this. I can't wait to put Damon's ass away for good this time."

"Can you get your mother or somebody else to go with you?"

"Jay, I'm good. I am meeting Taj and Faith."

"Let me call Roc," he insisted.

"Jay, I said I am good. Please just focus on Jordan, and tell him that I love him and that he is in my prayers. Are your parents already up there?"

"Yeah, Mom has been here all night. She said she's not going anywhere until she knows for sure that Jordan is okay. Pops left briefly, but he came right back. He is worried but is just trying to stay strong."

"Please send my love and call me after he gets out of surgery. He's going to be fine. I love you."

"I love you too, Joi. As soon as I know Jordan is okay, I am going down to the police station to file a complaint."

"We'll do whatever we need to do, but only after everything is fine with Jordan."

As I approached the police station, I started

having déjà vu about the last time I had to meet Roc down here. I looked over at the side of the station and saw Taj's car parked over in a corner. She was sitting inside it with Faith, waiting for me. I parked next to her and rolled down my window.

"Are you guys ready to go inside?" I asked.

"We sure are. The sooner Damon and Toni are off the streets, the sooner you can get your life back, Joi."

"Please don't call Eboni, you guys. I don't want her to worry. Besides, she has to stay focused," I said.

"With all of this going on, are you still going to Eboni's industry party?" Taj asked once we got out of the cars.

"I am sure that that is the last thing on her mind, Taj," Faith replied.

"I'm sorry. My nerves are just getting the best of me, so I was just trying to talk about something else," said Taj.

"It's okay. I want to go, but with everything that is going on with Jordan and all this mess with Toni and Damon, I just don't know," I explained.

"Yeah, Joi, you got your hands full, but hopefully after I talk to the police, they will arrest them," said Taj.

"I hope so, but I know how these things work. Damon could just say it's your word against his and Toni's," I replied.

"Well, luckily for me, I was able to record most of it on my BlackBerry," Taj revealed.

"Girl! Why didn't you tell me that when we talked earlier?" asked Faith.

"I know. I just wanted to wait until I saw you so that I could show you in person. I even sent a copy to my computer as backup. You know I'm nosy and that my cell goes everywhere with me," Taj confessed.

"Make sure you send me a copy, because you are good for losing your phone and having problems with your computer," Faith said.

Taj nodded. "You're absolutely right. I will send it to you now."

"Who thinks of stuff like that in that type of situation? I know I probably wouldn't," I said.

"All I did was press two buttons to record. I had a damn good angle, so you can see both of them in the video," Taj explained.

"Let me see," I said.

"Hold your horses." Taj slightly chuckled.

Taj pressed the button to play the video, and at first it looked like it was going up and down. Finally, you could see and hear Damon and Toni clearly talking about what had happened to Jordan. I was also surprised to hear how Damon was just threatening her. Toni was also confessing to some other incriminating activity, hacking into people's credit cards.

"Whoa. Joi, I know this chick just didn't say what I thought she said," Faith snarled.

"Hell, which part? Everything sounded crazy," I replied.

"She is just as crooked and conniving as he is," Taj added.

"They are two peas in a pod," I said.

"Hmmm. Soon they will be two peas doing time for the same crime," Faith said.

"They deserve everything they have coming to them," Taj said.

"Well, let's go inside and get this over with. Hopefully, they can pick their asses up tonight," I said.

We walked into the police station, and I recognized one of the detectives who had been a witness for the prosecution a few months ago.

"Hey, Joi. What are you doing down in this neck of the woods?" he said.

"Hi, Detective Johnson. We came down here to file a complaint," I replied.

"A complaint about what?" he asked.

"Attempted murder, conspiracy to commit a crime, fraud, you just name it," I told him.

"Well, have a seat and I will be right back," he said.

Detective Johnson and one of his colleagues took all three of us back into a room and took statements. Taj played the video on her cell phone, and they wanted to take her cell phone to use as evidence.

"You want to take my phone and use it for evidence?" Taj said.

"Why, yes. We need that video as evidence in this case," Detective Johnson responded.

"Can I send you a copy of the video?" Taj asked.

"Yes. Just e-mail it to the address on my business

card, and I will retrieve it in a few minutes,"
replied Detective Johnson.

"Whew, thank you, Jesus. I can't do anything
without my phone. You do understand, Joi?"
said Taj.

"Taj, I understand," I assured her.

Ring.

I looked down to see if it was Jaylen calling me,
and the screen said Vanessa I quickly excused
myself to take the call in the hallway.

"Hello, Vanessa?"

"Hi, Joi. How are you doing?"

"I'm doing fine," I lied. "So, are we still on for
this Friday?"

"Yes, we are. I will see you then," Vanessa confirmed.

She hung up the telephone, and I had this
strange feeling come over me. It wasn't a bad feeling, but I really couldn't explain it. I started walking back toward the room, and my telephone rang
again. This time it was Jaylen.

"Jay? Is everything all right?" I asked.

"Yeah, baby. He is still in surgery. The doctor
said that he would come out and give us an update
immediately after the surgery. I received a call
from Detective Johnson, and he is sending someone up here to talk to me in about an hour, so I'm
going to wait around up here. He wanted to come
now, but I told him that now was not a good time."

"I'm sure he understands that. I just spoke to
Detective Johnson a few minutes ago, and he is

all over it. We did some work together on a case about a year ago. He is pretty thorough."

"So how is it going?" Jaylen asked.

"Baby, Taj came through for us in such a huge way."

"How?"

"To make a long story short, she recorded everything Look, Jay, I have to go. Go and focus on Jordan, because he needs you now, and I will explain everything to you in detail later on. I love you."

"I love you, too."

I hung up the telephone and went back into the room. Detective Johnson said that he had a few more things he needed to run by his boss and then they would be issuing warrants for Damon's and Toni's arrest.

"I'm so glad that this is almost over with," Taj declared.

"Me, too. Joi, I don't know how you stay so strong," said Faith.

I shrugged. "Yeah, it is really putting a damper on my career. I can't concentrate on my work, and I am missing a lot of time. I need to put in for a leave of absence," I said.

"I don't know about y'all, but I need to start going back to church," Taj said.

"We all can go to church this Sunday," Faith suggested.

"Count me in, because I know that I need to go," Taj retorted.

"We need to go to church more than one

Sunday. With everything that has been going on, I personally need to go every day," Faith chuckled.

"Amen to that," I said. "Well, let's make it happen."

Finally, it seemed like all the craziness was coming to a halt. Right now I needed a strong dose of church. Jaylen and I had talked about finding a church home after we got married, but we just hadn't found the time to visit any of the ones that came highly recommended. All I knew was that we had had enough drama to last a lifetime. I'd figured that we would have to go through some drama, but not on this level. Damon and Toni were hopefully getting arrested tonight or tomorrow. I wished it was tonight, but I wouldn't complain. Vanessa had called to confirm our meeting. Hopefully, Jordan would make a full recovery. I had to confide in Roc—without Jaylen's knowledge—about my possible rape. I was devastated. I had to make an appointment with my ob-gyn to get an exam. I knew everything was not going to go as smoothly as I would like, but some of the storm was hopefully almost over.

Chapter 16

You Are the Father!

Roc

Rick contacted me to let me know that he had come across some information on Damon that I would be interested in knowing. I couldn't wait to see what he had, because time was running out. Damon's latest actions clearly told me that he was a ticking time bomb ready to explode. I just wanted to be done with all this craziness. Joi was my girl. She was like the sister I'd never had. It was hard to explain. So many of my friends used to tell me that they thought I was secretly attracted to her. I didn't want to ruin our friendship, so I would lay low just in case she thought the same way. I mean, don't get me wrong. Joi was the total package. She was smart, sassy, and did I mention beautiful? I just had great respect and admiration for her. Besides, she had never showed any interest in me. She had always told me that I was her brother from another mother.

That was neither here nor there now, because I had my sights set on her girl Faith. Man, I was feelin' her. That kiss had my head all messed up. I just hoped that she was for real, because I would love to treat her like the queen she was. But for now, my job was to investigate Damon. I told Rick to meet me at the office because I was expecting some faxes to come over. Several minutes later, I walked through the door and saw Rick just standing there.

"Man, we have been robbed. Look at this place. Shit is everywhere," Rick snapped.

"Damn, what the fuck happened, yo? Did you call the police?"

"Not yet. I got here just five minutes before you."

"I'll call," I said.

Ring.

"Police, fire, and ambulance. Dispatcher two-four-one. How may I help you?"

"Yes, I need to report a break-in at two-oh-seven Main Street, second floor."

"And your name, sir?"

"Roc Davenport."

I finished giving the dispatcher the additional information that he requested. Within fifteen minutes of hanging up, several police cars pulled up. Once the officers were inside, Rick answered most of the questions since he had been the first on the scene. I was pissed because there were papers everywhere. It looked like someone tried to pry open my main file cabinet. But, unless you could drag that cabinet out of the building and shoot it up, there was no way you were going to be able to get to those files.

"Do you know of anyone who would want to break into your office?" asked one of the officers.

"Yeah, Damon Grant," I replied.

"You mean Damon Grant, the ex-football player?" asked the officer.

"No other," I said.

"Why would you think that?"

"Because I had a small run-in with him the other day over a personal issue," I explained.

"Well, thanks for the lead. We will be sure to follow up on it. We also have a warrant for his arrest," said the officer.

I nodded. "That's good to know."

The police stayed for approximately forty-five more minutes, collecting information and possible evidence, and then they took off. There was no way in hell I was going to stick around and fix this office up right now. I would just return tomorrow, early in the a.m., to get started.

"Well, count me in. I should be here by eight in the morning," Rick assured me.

"Before you leave, where is the information that you had for me on Damon?"

"Oh, snap, my bad. Here you go. You might want to sit down for this one," Rick replied.

I took some documents out of the manila folder and separated everything on my desk. As I started looking through some of the stuff, I was quickly drawn to a copy of Damon's birth certificate. The name read Henry Damon Grant. Mother, Delores Grant. Father, Henry Payne.

"Henry Payne? I wonder if he is related to Jaylen Payne," I said.

"Did you see the name on that birth certificate?" Rick asked.

"Are you thinking what I'm thinking?"

"What is Jaylen's pop's first name?"

"I can't remember. I've just always called him Mr. Payne," I said.

"Why don't you call somebody who might know?" asked Rick.

"That's a good idea. I'll ask Faith. She has known Joi and Jaylen for years."

Ring.

Click . . . click.

"Hello, Faith."

"Oh, hi, Roc. I thought you were going to be calling me later on?"

"Yeah, I am, but I wanted to ask you something real quick."

"What?"

"What is Jaylen's father's name?" I asked.

"Uh, I call him Mr. Henry sometimes, and sometimes I call him Mr. Payne. Why?"

"It's not important. I just wanted to send them a card."

"That's so sweet. Well, I have to finish cooking dinner."

"Is that an invitation?"

"Wait and see when you call," Faith teased.

"I'll do that. Talk to you in a few."

"So what's the verdict?" Rick asked.

"His first name is Henry, but I don't want to jump to any conclusions. Henry Payne is a common name. I need to find out if Delores Grant has a picture or something that would link the two of them together. If Damon turns out to be Jaylen and Jordan's brother, shit is going to hit the fan."

From that moment on, I knew that I was going to have to handle this newfound information with caution. I needed to be absolutely sure. I wished I could go straight to the source and ask Mr. Payne if he knew a Delores Grant, but with everything that was going on with his son Jordan, now was definitely not the best time. But time was of the essence, and I had to find out one way or the other.

I reached out to Joi to see if she wouldn't mind contacting her father-in-law and asking him to call me. He called me later that same evening. I explained to him what it was that I did for a living and that I had come across some information that might be of interest. He said that he remembered me from the wedding, and he agreed to meet me at my home office tomorrow at nine in the morning. I gave him the address, along with the directions.

The next morning.

Mr. Payne arrived right on time. Dude was sharp. He pulled up driving a new white Jaguar luxury sedan. He got out of the vehicle and approached the front entrance to my home.

"Hello, Mr. Payne. Thanks for agreeing to meet with me. I know that your family has been dealing with a lot lately, and I am glad that Jordan is doing better."

"Thanks, son. My wife and I couldn't be happier. That was a close call, but God is so good."

"Yes, he is. All the time," I replied.

"So you said that you wanted to talk to me about something important, so let's talk."

"Well, I was doing some research for Joi, and I came across some information that was a little confusing, to say the least," I explained as I showed Mr. Payne into the living room.

"And what does this information have to do with me?"

"Well, can you tell me whether or not you know a woman by the name of Delores Grant?" I asked.

"Why, why, yes, I do, but I haven't seen her in years," he nervously responded.

"Did she live in the Northeast?"

"Why do you want to know about Delores? That was a long time ago."

"With all due respect, Mr. Payne, some information has surfaced linking you directly to Delores Grant."

"Just stop beating around the bush and tell me what information has surfaced."

"She listed you as the father of her son on a birth certificate," I disclosed.

Mr. Payne looked like he had seen a ghost. For

a few seconds, he just stood there, and then he started mumbling to himself like he could not believe it.

"Let me see the birth certificate," he said.

"Here you go, sir."

He grabbed the certificate and started perusing the form in pure disbelief. He took off his hat and just started pacing the floors back and forth. Afterward, he took out his eyeglasses and put them on and then looked at the birth certificate again. What was even stranger was that Damon had a strong resemblance to Mr. Payne.

"Oh, Lord. What did I do? I didn't know. I didn't know," he said.

"Well, your son does not go by Henry. He goes by Damon Grant. Does it ring a bell?"

"The only Damon Grant I know played for the Philadelphia Eagles."

"Bingo."

"Get the hell outta here. There's no way. There is just no way," he repeated.

"Well, there is a lot more going on that you do not know, Mr. Payne," I revealed.

"Give me a minute to digest this."

"Take all the time you need."

"Where is Delores? I need to see her for myself. And where is Damon? I need to meet him and explain so much. I am going to have to explain all of this to my family, but I don't know where to begin."

"Mr. Payne, we have a much more complex

situation going on with Damon and some other members of your family."

"Like what?"

"We have reason to believe that Damon is responsible for what happened to Jordan," I explained.

"What in the hell do you mean, he is responsible for what happened to Jordan?"

"I know none of this makes sense right now, but after you speak with Jaylen and Joi, they will fill in the missing blanks."

Mr. Payne shook his head. "I can't tell my son about this. He just got married, and his twin brother is recovering from surgery. I won't do it."

"Well, if you don't tell him, I will. There is a maniac loose out there, and his name is Damon. There is just so much that you do not know. He hates Jaylen and Joi. He was at their wedding, and he is stalking Joi wherever she goes."

"How do you know this?"

"I know this because I had to pull him off of her at Cherry Hill Mall last week," I replied.

I sat Mr. Payne down and filled him in on everything. He finally came to grips with it and refocused his energy on helping Jaylen and Joi. He was in total shock. He wanted me to set up a meeting with Miss Delores. I told him that I would be in touch with him tomorrow to set up a meeting with Miss Delores. I wanted to check with Faith first to see if it was okay.

* * *

Later that evening

Ring.
Click.

"Hello, Roc. I'm glad you called," Faith said with a smile on her face.

"I told you that I would, and I am a man of my word," I said.

"I see. I see. So are you in the neighborhood?"

"I can be. Why do you ask?"

"Well, I whipped up a little suthin', suthin' for dinner, and I wanted to invite you over."

"Are you going to try and take advantage of me?" I teased.

"No, I am not."

"Damn. I was hoping that you would," I replied.

"Let's see how the night plays out."

Chapter 17

The Reunion

Faith

After speaking with Roc last night, I went to work with a lot of mixed feelings about Miss Delores seeing Jaylen's father again. It had been over thirty years, and I didn't want her to have a setback. I decided to speak to her psychologist regarding the matter. She wanted to talk to Miss Delores with me present to feel her out first. The psychologist's take on things was that it might be good for Miss Delores to move on by bringing closure to that chapter in her life. I contacted Mr. Payne to see when he could stop by. He told me that he was on his way up to the hospital to see his son. That worked out perfect.

"I need for you to make my hair look pretty. Okay?" said Miss Delores.

"Of course, Miss Delores. I am also going to put a little make-up on your face and lips," I told her.

"Nurse Faith, now don't get me in any trouble." She laughed.

Within an hour, Mr. Payne arrived at the hospital. I pulled him over to the side and explained to him Miss Delores's present state of mind. He said that he understood and would exercise good judgment and care. After I finished fixing up Miss Delores's hair and make-up, I took her into a smaller room so that she could see Mr. Henry Payne. As she waited for him to enter the room, she looked over at me and winked her eye. Mr. Payne walked over to her and softly called her name. He grabbed her hand, and they hugged each other. Tears overflowed on both of their faces, so I went and gave them both some tissue. I needed some, too, because it looked like a scene out of a romance novel.

"Delores, you look great. You haven't changed a bit," Mr. Payne said, with a huge smile on his face.

"You don't look so bad yourself," she responded.

"Boy, do we have a lot to talk about," said Mr. Payne.

"Nurse Faith, would it be all right if we had some privacy for a few minutes? And don't worry I won't end up pregnant like before," said Miss Delores.

"Take all the time you need," I told them.

They talked for over two hours. The staff brought in food from the cafeteria, and they played checkers and talked. He showed her pictures of his family, and surprisingly, she had some old pictures of Damon when he was a kid. I didn't know what he told her, but she was definitely glowing. Mr. Payne came over and gave me a hug before he left and told me to keep taking real good care of her.

"Wow, Miss Delores, you are blushing," I said after Mr. Payne had gone.

"Did you see that man? Lord, if he wasn't married, I would have major plastic surgery just so that I would look like Alicia Keys or somebody like her."

"You are so crazy. Did you have a good conversation?"

Miss Delores nodded. "Yes, we did. I told him about the letters that I wrote to him, but I didn't have a recent address to mail them to. We talked about Henry Jr., and he wants to meet him."

"Do you think that is a good idea?"

"Yes, I do. It wasn't his fault. He didn't know. I forgave him. We are good friends now. I'm going to tell Henry today that his father wants to finally meet him. He said that he could stop by the house later on."

"I'm so happy for you," I said.

"Now, if I could only find my two brothers and my baby girl, who I gave up for adoption, I would be the happiest person in the whole wide world."

"That would be nice, but let's do one thing at a time," I told her.

Miss Delores
Back at Miss Delores's home.

"Henry? Henry, can you come into the room so that I can talk to you?"

"In a minute, Mom," Damon called.

"Well, hurry up. It's important," I said. "Henry? I have somebody that I want you to meet."

"My name is Damon, not Henry, and I really do not have time to meet anybody."

"Henry! Please listen to me. I need for you to come and meet your father."

"Am I being punked?" Damon bellowed.

"No, Henry, you're not. He will be here in a minute."

Damon shuffled into the living room. "Mom, please don't do this. I'm not ready."

"Please, son, I need for you to be ready for me."

"Well, what about me? This m - - - has never been a part of my life, and now he wants to know me?" Damon yelled.

"Honey, he didn't know about you. Please calm down, or you are going to make me have a nervous breakdown."

"I knew about him. Shit, I went up to him at a football game and introduced myself," Damon shouted. "It seemed like I was talking to myself. He didn't even know it was me. Where was his fatherly intuition?"

"Well, calm down, Damon. He is about to come through the door."

Just then the doorbell rang. I ran to the front door and showed Henry into the house. Henry walked into the room and looked Damon up and down. He knew most everything that Damon had done, and he could not control his emotions. His whole body language changed. He was furious.

As much as he wanted to contain his emotions, he just couldn't.

"You bastard! You tried to murder my son Jordan," Henry shouted.

"Henry! Please let him go. This is crazy. You're upsetting me," I said.

"Damn you. Like I said, you're not my father, so go back and be there for your other two sons," Damon yelled.

"Did you know that Jaylen and Jordan were your half brothers?" asked Henry.

"Uh, let's see. Something like that," Damon taunted.

"What in the hell is wrong with you? Jordan is your half brother, and you show absolutely no remorse for almost killing him?" Henry thundered.

Damon narrowed his eyes. "And your point?"

"You're one sick individual. Hate me all you want, but your brothers have nothing to do with how you feel about me," Henry shouted.

"So what? After all these years, I'm supposed to welcome you with open arms?" Damon retorted.

"Look, son, I heard you, and I didn't know that your mother was pregnant," Henry said. "I bent over backward to make our relationship work. I loved your mother. I apologize for so many things, but if I failed to recognize you in person as my son, then I am truly sorry, but that doesn't give you the right to go around and hurt innocent people."

"So now you know. What in the hell do you want from me?" Damon asked.

"I don't want anything from you. I don't hate you, but I don't really give a damn about your feelings right now," Henry growled.

Damon rolled his eyes. "Good riddance. You're a day late and a dollar short, anyway."

"That's your choice, but if you ever try to hurt another member of my family, father or not, you will regret it. I promise you that, punk," Henry warned.

"Hey, guys, please stop fighting," I pleaded.

"Delores, it was not my intention to come over here to upset you. Please accept my apology," said Henry.

Toni overheard some noise in the room and took it upon herself to walk in to see what was going on. "Damon, I heard a lot of noise. Is everything all right?"

"Toni?" Henry asked, looking pissed off and confused.

"Uh, um, hello, Mr. Payne," said Toni.

"What the hell are you doing here?" Henry asked.

"That is Damon's girlfriend, Henry. How do you know her?" I inquired.

"Toni is my ex-daughter-in-law. She was married to my son Jaylen," Henry explained.

"Oh, really? What a small world," I said.

"Yeah, too small," Henry groaned.

"Toni, can you please excuse us?" Damon insisted.

Toni nodded. "No problem. I will be in the other room."

I was a little confused with everything going on

at this point, but I just wanted to make things right with Damon and his father, Henry. From what I was hearing, it sounded like my son had some more siblings. It also sounded like he was maybe in a lot of trouble.

"Henry, maybe you can come back another time," I said. "This is not going all that well. Besides, I need to talk to Damon alone. I am sorry about everything, and I will keep your son in my prayers. Is that okay?"

"I understand, Delores. I apologize for my outburst. Here. Please take my number. We'll talk soon," Henry replied. "Damon, until you come to terms with your actions and take responsibility for those actions, I don't want to have anything to do with you. Stay the hell away from my family."

When Henry closed the front door behind him, I turned to Damon.

"Henry Damon Grant, what has gotten into you? As soon as I think I am getting on with my life, you ruin it. What have you done now? I have to go and get myself together. You know I can't deal with all this mess. I need to call my doctor."

"That man is only a sperm donor to me. I hate him."

"Oh, Lord, this boy is about to make me have another nervous breakdown. Please don't do this," I begged.

"All he cares about is those two twin boys of his. I hope they both die."

"Damon, you don't mean that. Why are you so bitter?"

"Because when I needed him, he wasn't there," Damon replied. "He broke your heart and made you have a nervous breakdown. I basically had to fetch for myself without a father, and look at me now. He never came to any of my football games, whether it was college or professional, as my father. I never had a father figure to talk to. You are damn right, Mom. I am bitter, and please don't say he didn't know. He knew he slept with you, so he should have checked."

"Miss Delores, I need to tell you something," said Toni, who had come back into the room.

"Toni, you definitely don't want to go there, or I promise you that it will be a long time before you see your little boy again," Damon growled.

"Damon, I can't keep living like this. The walls are falling in on us. If you can't trust your mother, then who can you trust? She loves you," Toni replied.

"Tell me what, Toni? What has Henry Damon done?" I asked.

"You'd better not say one word, Toni, or I will make sure you regret it," Damon said in a threatening tone.

"Henry Damon, you are all I have, so if you are in any trouble, please tell me so that I can help you," I pleaded.

"We both hurt Jordan," Toni blurted out.

"I gathered that much, Toni. What did you do, and why?" I said.

"Damon meant to hurt Jaylen, but his twin brother, Jordan, got caught in the middle."

As Toni started explaining her version, Damon slammed the door and left. I could tell that she was scared of my son. As I went to call my doctor, I thought about calling Nurse Faith. But what would I tell her? I did not know who to call or what to do. My son had just come back home, and I didn't want him to leave me again. I hated living alone. I would call Henry; he'd know what to do.

Ring. Click, click.

"Hello? Who is calling?"

"Henry, this is Delores. Are you busy?"

"Well, actually I am. I am up here at the hospital, visiting my son Jordan. You sound upset. Is everything all right?"

"Not really. It's Damon."

"What happened?"

"It's just so much, Henry. Damon knows a lot more about your family than he said earlier. I also know that girl Toni has something to do with it. She's bad news, too."

"I already know, Delores."

"What happened to your son?"

"I will tell you later. I just have a lot to absorb."

Henry hung up the telephone so fast, I didn't get a chance to tell him that Damon had left.

Chapter 18

The Arrest

Miss Delores

Ring. Click.

"Hello, Miss Delores. Is everything all right?"

"No, Nurse Faith, and I don't know what to do. Damon has gone crazy, and he and this girl Toni hurt somebody," I sobbed.

"Miss Delores, where is Mr. Henry?" Faith asked.

"He left, but I just called him, and he is going to stop back over shortly."

"Just calm down, Miss Delores. I am on my way."

"Hurry please."

My son Damon came back into the house and started yelling at Toni. I thought he was going to hit her. I could hear her crying and saying that she was sorry. All I could hear were doors slamming open and shut. It sounded like Damon was packing up to leave.

"Damon, where are you going?" I said.

"I'm sorry, Mom, but I have to leave for a while. I just left my job, and that stupid m - - - Orlando told me that I was no longer allowed on the premises, or he would call the police for trespassing. There are just a lot of things going on right now. Don't worry. I will be back."

"What do you mean you will be back? You just got here," I said.

Knock, knock.

"Miss Delores, it's me, Nurse Faith."

"Come in," I yelled.

"Miss Delores, why are you crying? Please come over here and sit down. I'll go and get you some water," said Faith.

"What the hell are you doing in my house, Faith?" Damon yelled.

"I am your mother's nurse and she called me. She needs to calm down, Damon. Your mother is not strong enough to handle all of this. She is going to have a relapse. Her hands are clammy, and she does not look well. I am really concerned."

Twenty minutes later.

Knock, knock.

"Who in the hell is it now?" Damon complained.

Faith ran to the door and invited Henry inside.

"It's me, Henry Payne. Your mother just called me. What in the hell is going on in there? Where is she?"

"Hi, Mr. Payne. I am a friend of Joi's and also

Miss Delores's nurse. Look, I need to get her out of here, away from all of this," Faith explained. "I just called my friend Roc. He is aware of everything. He is also bringing the police to talk to Damon and Toni. I hate to be the one to tell you this, but Jordan's car accident was planned."

"Are they on their way now?" Henry asked.

"Yes, they will be here shortly. I am taking her outside," said Faith.

"You both intentionally planned to hurt my damn son?" Henry shouted at Damon and Toni.

"Man, get the hell out of my way. I owe you nothing," Damon growled.

"He's your brother, you damn fool," Henry yelled.

"Oh, I know that, Pops." Damon snorted. "This wasn't no ordinary coincidence that I ended up in this part of town. I came here on purpose. Before and after my career ended, I desperately wanted to meet you. Hell, I wanted to meet you all my life. I did my research and made a lot of phone calls. It wasn't hard to find you, but when I met you for the first time, you rejected me."

Henry shook his head. "How did I reject you? I didn't know who you were!"

"A father should just know."

"Said the man who has yet to be a father. That is the most ridiculous thing I've ever heard."

"The only children you ever cared about were your twin sons, Jordan and Jaylen. Well, where were you when I needed you?"

"Had you told me, I would have accepted you into my family. You're my son."

"All I ever wanted was to get to know my father. Damn the NFL. I would have traded places with anybody. My whole life has been screwed up from day one. Mom was on drugs, and she had different men coming in and out of the house. I was abused in foster home after foster home. Do you know how many times I begged for you to come and get me? Do you understand what I'm telling you? I lost my dignity and self-respect a long time ago, so go ahead and tell me how disappointed you are in me. I tell myself that every day."

"You haven't lost me, son. But feeling sorry for yourself is not going to make things better for you. Just turn yourself in, and I will help you."

"Damon, come on. The police are on their way. We need to get the hell out of here," Toni pleaded.

"How did you hook up with Toni? Never mind. I don't even want to know," said Henry.

"She belonged to Jaylen at one point, just like Joi. I found out that Jaylen was Joi's college sweetheart, and when they broke up, I made my move," Damon explained. "I knew exactly where she worked, and I pursued her. The only problem was that I fell in love with her, but she wasn't in love with me, and you have no idea how much I hate rejection. I bumped into Toni at Joi and Jaylen's wedding, and the rest is history. She doesn't mean anything to me. I just used her."

"You used me? You son of a bitch. I used you, too," Toni yelled.

Toni grabbed her pocketbook and stormed

through the back door. I could see sirens and police cars out on the front lawn.

"Officer, one of the people you are looking for is Toni, and she just went out the back door. She was also involved in the attempted murder of Jordan Payne," Roc explained.

"Well, I just checked, and she is not in the backyard. She must have slipped away," said the officer.

"Well, she needs to be found right away and locked the hell up," Roc said.

Faith

I greeted Roc as Miss Delores sat in the car. She had been very upset but she had managed to calm down. She'd said that she was experiencing tightness in her chest, so I'd checked her blood pressure and other vital signs. For now, she was stable, but I knew that I needed to get her away from all this commotion. I had called the ambulance earlier so that she could get checked out by a doctor. The police were questioning Damon regarding the whereabouts of Toni. Finally, the ambulance pulled up, and Miss Delores was placed inside. Out of nowhere, Damon sprinted over to the ambulance to check on his mother. He hastily walked over to the back door and gave her a long hug and a kiss. He reassured her that this was not as bad as it seemd and that he would be all right.

As he turned around, the police escorted him over to a squad car to read him his rights.

"Damon Payne, you are under arrest for the attempted murder of Jordan Payne. You have the right to remain silent. Anything you say can and will be used against you in a court of law. You have the right to an attorney. If you can't afford one, one will be appointed to you for representation. You can exercise your rights not to answer any questions or make any statements. Do you understand your rights?"

"Yes," Damon mumbled.

They put handcuffs on him and hauled him off to the station. Roc said that the police were still searching for Toni. Roc said that he had found out some good news on Miss Delores's daughter and her two brothers. Apparently, her daughter lived in Upper Marlboro, Maryland, and had been there her entire life. She had a husband and three children. She had already been contacted by social services, and she was excited about meeting her mother for the first time. Miss Delores's two brothers were actually living in an assisted-living facility in New York. They still needed to be contacted.

Mr. Payne was slowly walking out of the house, shaking his head.

"Mr. Payne, are you going to be okay?" I asked.

"Yes, Faith, I will be just fine. I just need to go to the hospital and check on Jordan. Once everything calms down, I will speak to my family."

"I hope that you know that none of this is your fault," I said.

"Yeah, I know, but I just didn't know what I was walking into. I'm going to be leaving now. Can you please call me later and let me know how Delores is doing?"

"Well, they just took her to the hospital. Maybe you can call and check on her over there. Aren't you going over to the hospital to check on Jordan, anyway?"

"You're right. You kids, take care. I need to call Jaylen, anyway, and let him know everything that just happened."

Thirty minutes later.

I called Joi and told her everything. She was in disbelief, but she was happy about Damon's arrest. I told her that Toni had slipped through the back door, but that they had put out an APB for her arrest as well.

"I'm so glad that I don't have to explain about Mr. Henry being Damon's father. Now that's some crazy mess," said Joi. "I know that Mrs. Payne is going to flip out when she hears this. But then again, it did happen before he met her."

"Well, we'll talk tomorrow. I need to get up to the hospital and check on Miss Delores. I was supposed to be cooking dinner for Roc, but with all this drama, dinner was over before it started cooking."

"Boy, Eboni, is missing all the action."

"Lucky her," I remarked.

"She'll be home next weekend. Hopefully, you can make it to her industry party, or whatever you call it."

"Yeah, I could use a night out. We should go over to open mic tonight. We can do a quickie celebration of Damon's arrest. Now you don't have to worry about his ass stalking you."

"You know that might just work. Let me see how long Jaylen is going to be up at the hospital," said Joi.

"I tell you what. You go and check on your husband, and I will go and check on Miss Delores. Let's meet up around nine thirty tonight. Also, call Taj and see if she wants to come and celebrate. She really came through for you."

"Yes, she did."

Joi called Taj and Jaylen as I went to check on Miss Delores. By the time I got there, Mr. Henry was just leaving her side in the emergency room.

"They just admitted her. She is right over there. They want to keep her overnight for observation," he told me.

"I think that is a great idea," I said.

I followed transportation as they escorted her to her room. I held her hand on the elevator, and I helped get her settled into her bed.

"Thanks for coming, Nurse Faith. You treat me so good. I love you," said Miss Delores.

"I love you, too, Miss Delores."

"Where is Damon?"

"He's all right. They just want to talk to him down at the station," I replied.

"I sure hope so. I know he got issues, but I do love him. Had my mind been right, I would have tracked down Henry to let him know he had a son. Who knows, we could have been married by now."

"Just get some rest tonight. Besides, I may have some good news for you in the morning."

"Like what?" Miss Delores asked.

"Not tonight. Get some sleep." I kissed her forehead and turned out the light.

I met up with Joi and Taj at 9:30. We went over to open mic to celebrate. Roc called me to see if I wanted to meet up later on. I told him that I was going out with Joi and Taj to celebrate. I invited him, but he nicely declined and promised to call me later. He said that he had some loose ends to tie up with the break-in at his office and everything that had happened to Damon and Toni.

We parked the car and went inside. As soon as we walked in, Dre immediately walked over to personally escort us to our seats.

"So what brings you ladies by?" he asked.

"We're sorta, kinda celebrating," I said.

"So, Faith, are you going to grace us with your presence on the mic?" Dre asked.

"I'm not sure. I'm still thinking about it," I replied.

"Well, if you change your mind, just let me know," Dre said, sounding hopeful.

"Can you send over a waitress so that we can order some drinks?" I asked.

"What do you need, Faith? I'll put in your order," Dre offered.

"Can you bring us three apple martinis, or appletinis?" I asked.

"They will be right up," said Dre.

"Thanks, Dre."

The place wasn't that crowded tonight, but there were a few people in the audience. The poetry was a little edgy, but I didn't mind. The only poetry that gets on my nerves is that militant junk. The waitress returned shortly with our drinks, and I gave a toast in honor of Joi in regards to Damon's arrest.

"Good riddance to Damon," I shouted.

"I hope he drops dead," Joi said with a cold, straight stare.

"I'll toast to that. We'll have to celebrate again once they arrest Toni," Taj said.

"So, Taj, on a lighter note, what's going on with you and Orlando? When are we going to formally meet him?" I asked.

"Well, Joi already met him at the gym," Taj replied.

"Oh yeah, that's real formal. Why don't you two come over for dinner? I mean, is it serious?" Faith inquired.

"Not really, guys. We're just taking it one day at a time, but I do like him," said Taj.

"Well, Roc and I have been spending some time together lately," I announced.

"Wow, Faith. I'm so happy for you. I tried to flirt with him once, but he didn't bite, so I just kept it moving," Taj retorted.

"I hope you guys plan on going to Eboni's party. You know, she is our girl and she needs our support," I said.

"Faith, please be quiet. You know that you want to go to be nosy and see if anybody famous is going to be there," Joi responded.

"That's not a crime, is it? This is our first industry party, so I just cannot miss it. So are you guys in or out?" I said.

"Count us in," Joi and Taj simultaneously responded.

"Are we still going to church this Sunday?" Joi asked.

"I plan on it. I need to go and get some prayer," I said. "What about you, Taj?"

"I will be dressed with bells on. I need Jesus in my life," Taj proclaimed.

"Well, I need a prayer and a miracle," Joi said.

"And forgiveness for wishing someone dead," I retorted.

"What the hell ever, Faith," Joi returned.

We finished up our drinks and stayed to listen to a few more poets. I needed to get some rest because I had to get to work early and check on Miss Delores. Joi just wanted to get home to her husband, and Taj was staying over at Orlando's. I could tell that Joi was not herself. Her mind was constantly drifting off, and her mood went from one extreme to the next.

As soon as I got home, I took a shower and got ready for bed. What a long and draining day!

Chapter 19

Change of Heart

Joi

Today was the day that I would meet up with Vanessa at the Bonefish Grill. I had a good feeling about this meeting. It just had to be good news. I was meeting up with her in about an hour, so I needed to finish getting dressed. Jaylen had rushed out of the house early this morning. He had left a note saying he was going over to his parents' house. I could only imagine what that meeting was about. Although I did not want to be there, I needed to check on Jaylen to see if he needed me.

Ring.

"Hello, Jaylen?"

"Hey, baby. Are you getting ready to leave for your meeting?"

"In about thirty minutes. So did your dad talk to you and your mom yet?"

"Yeah, he did," said Jaylen. "He explained everything the best he could. I just cannot believe that I am related to that asshole. He will never be a brother of mines."

"How is your mother holding up?" I asked.

"She's fine. She is not upset with Dad, because all of this happened years before they met and he didn't know. Plus, her focus is on Jordan right now, and although he is getting stronger every day, she is not going to put too much more on her plate right now."

After I hung up with Jaylen, I called Faith to see what was going on.

Ring. Click.

"Hello, Faith. Are you at work?"

"Yeah, I've been here since seven thirty this morning. I had to speak to Miss Delores about some personal stuff."

"Oh, you can't discuss it?" I asked.

"Well, under the circumstances, I guess I can, because it is good news. I told Miss Delores that we had found her daughter and she was on her way to the hospital this afternoon to meet her. Plus, Roc found out that her two brothers are living in an assisted-living facility in New York."

"How did she take the news?"

"Well, at first I wasn't sure if I should have told her, but she was ecstatic," said Faith.

"So did she say anything about her son Damon?"

"Not one word since I told her about her daughter and her two brothers."

"Wow! Unbelievable."

"Well, I asked the psychologist about it, and he said that sometimes when a patient is dealing with posttraumatic stress, they bury the part that they cannot deal with at the time. Obviously, she cannot deal with Damon right now," Faith explained.

"I can relate to that," I replied.

"Joi, when you get a chance later on today, we need to talk. Something just ain't right, and I know you got a lot going on but there is something else you are not telling me."

"Wow, look at how fast the time has passed. I have to go and meet up with Vanessa. Keep me posted on Miss Delores's situation. Wish me luck and we will talk later."

"Good luck," Faith said.

I was only ten minutes away from the Bonefish Grill. I arrived five minutes early and started looking for Vanessa. She got there two minutes later, and she was definitely alone. I beeped the horn to let her know that I was there. We met at the front entrance of the restaurant.

"Hello, Vanessa."

"Hello, Joi. How are you doing?"

"As well as can be expected," I replied nervously.

We found some seats located in the back of the restaurant. We ordered a couple of raspberry iced teas and a shrimp cocktail.

"So what's the verdict, Vanessa? Marcus is Wil's son, isn't he?" I asked.

"Yes, Joi, he is, but he doesn't know about Wil. That's why I didn't say anything."

"So where does that leave my family? What happened?"

Vanessa went on to explain to me that after Wil died, she fell into a deep depression, which caused her to have a nervous breakdown. Her parents were concerned because of the baby she was carrying. She said that Wil had broken it off with Kendal because he and Vanessa were getting back together. They had started seeing each other earlier on, and she got pregnant on his last visit home. He told her that Kendal was crazy and was starting all these rumors about him, telling people that he had beaten her and all sorts of other stuff.

Wil had already had a run-in with her supposed ex-boyfriend Mack in the past, but the situation had escalated. Kendal told Mack that Wil had hit her, and before the party that night, Mack threatened him. Wil had called Vanessa that night, before he'd gone to the party, and she had begged him not to go. She had even called some of his teammates, but Wil had insisted on going. His last words to her were, "I love you. Take care of my son or daughter." Mack approached him and asked him why he had hit his girl, Kendal. They exchanged words, and then Mack pulled out a gun and shot at Wil. The bullet struck Wil and he died. The fact that Mack got off scot-free sent Vanessa overboard.

"Your brother was my life, and when Mack took

his life, he took all that I had in me," Vanessa explained.

"So Wil knew that you were pregnant with his child?" I asked.

"Yes, he did, Joi, and so did Kendal."

"So what's our next move?" I asked.

"Well, I thought about it, and I talked it over with my husband. And he agreed that we should tell Marcus the truth. He is almost grown now. We want to talk to him tonight."

"So if you tell him tonight, how soon can we introduce him to the family?"

"That's up to him. I will have to let you know how our talk goes. Is that fair?"

"Yes, it is, and thanks," I said.

We finished our appetizers and drinks. We sat around for about another hour and talked about current events and old neighborhood gossip.

"Well, I have to go now," Vanessa said.

"Call me tonight. It does not matter what time."

"Don't worry. I will."

After Vanessa pulled off, I clearly understood why she needed to handle things this way. Wil's death had had a major impact on her as well. I wished they could have stayed together, and then maybe my brother would be here with us now. Boy, what I would do to have my brother back.

I went up to the hospital to see Jordan, and surprisingly, he was sitting up and eating on his own.

"Jordan! How's my baby brother-in-law?" I said.

"Hey, Joi. What's got you in such a good mood?" Jordan asked.

"I'm just happy to see you, that's all. Where is Jaylen?"

"He left with Dad to go down to the police station. I guess it has something to do with Damon. He said that he would be back shortly and that if you stopped by for me, to watch you."

"Then I guess that I am in good hands."

"Hey, what can I say?" Jordan replied.

It was good to see Jordan sitting up, talking smack, and now he was babysitting me for Jaylen. I wanted to share my good news with Jaylen so bad, I was about to burst, but I still couldn't shake that horrible nightmare of the other night. It had to be a dream. I stayed to visit with Jordan until Mrs. Payne came by to see her son.

"Hello, Joi. Isn't God good? My baby is doing so much better."

"Hi, Mom. You look great. Did you get some rest?" said Jordan.

"For the first time in over a week," Mrs. Payne happily sighed.

"Well, I have to run out to the store and grab my mother a birthday present. Her birthday is this Sunday," I announced.

"Henry told me everything last night, Joi," Mrs. Payne whispered.

"Crazy, isn't it?" I replied.

"Who would have thought? My Henry? We still have to talk some more about it," said Mrs. Payne.

"Well, call me if you need me," I said.

I left Jordan's room and walked over to Faith's department. I wanted to see how things were going with Miss Delores. I went up to the unit clerk's desk and asked if they could page Faith for me. Soon after, Faith came walking around the corner, with this huge smile on her face.

"Wow, you are smiling from ear to ear. How is Miss Delores?" I said.

"She is going to be just fine," Faith replied. "Her daughter showed up with her husband and three kids. She had enough information on her mother to go to court and prove that Miss Delores was her birth mother. She said that she had been looking for her mother for a while. She didn't know that she had a brother or any other relatives. I gave her the information as to where she could find her uncles in New York."

"Did Miss Delores have any doubts?" I asked.

"Not one. Her daughter resembles a younger version of her. After she met her grandchildren, the rest was a wrap. Her daughter wants her to come and live with them in Maryland."

"So what is she going to do?"

Faith shrugged. "She is not sure. She wants to go to New York to see her two brothers first. Because she knows them, she may want to stay there if she can. She does not want to go back to the house alone. Her daughter and son-in-law promised to take her home tomorrow if the doctors give her the okay."

"I am so happy for her," I remarked.

"Well, I have to get back to work. By the way, when are you going back to work, Joi?"

"Soon. I took an emergency leave of absence. Hopefully, I will return in a couple of weeks. With everything that has been going on with Damon and stuff, I had to call my office and request some time off."

"I will be stopping by later. I need to know what is going on with my best friend, and I will not take no for an answer," Faith asserted.

"You got yourself a date."

I left the hospital and drove back home. I had to tell somebody about my nightmare, and the only person I trusted right now was Faith. She would know what to do. As I turned the key and went into the house, I noticed that the lock on the door looked like it had been tampered with. I stared at it for a few minutes to make sure that I wasn't overreacting. I would have Jay look at it when he got home. After walking into the house, I noticed that there was another dozen roses from Jaylen on the table.

The note read: *Thinking of you. Love, Jaylen.*

I looked down and saw my cell phone blinking. I had two messages. I dialed my code, and there was a message from Jaylen and one from Vanessa. Vanessa asked me to call her as soon as I retrieved her message. I had to step back and take a deep breath. My hands had started trembling again. I dialed Vanessa back first.

Ring. Click.

"Hello, Joi. I have some good news," Vanessa

said. "Marcus wants to meet you guys. He wasn't upset or anything. I was surprised, because I just thought it would be a great idea to have him meet you first and then ease in the rest of the family but you know how teenagers are these days. I was just wondering what day works for you, because he actually wanted to come over there today."

"I can't believe it. I don't know what to say. As much as I want to see him today, can he wait until tomorrow afternoon? Tomorrow is my mother's birthday. What a surprise this would be for her to meet her only grandson."

"I agree. It's a date. I will see you tomorrow at two."

"Okay. Bye and thanks again," I said.

Now I needed to call Jaylen to tell him the good news. He wasn't going to believe it.

Ring. Click.

"Hi, Jay. Thanks for the beautiful flowers. Where are you?"

"You are welcome, and I'm on my way home to see my beautiful wife."

"I need to stop by the mall to get Mom a present for her birthday tomorrow. I also need to pick up something extra for a surprise guest."

"Who?" Jaylen asked.

"I will fill you in later at home. So what is the deal with Toni and Damon?"

"They are charging both of them with attempted murder, fraud, and a few more things. It's crazy. Toni has not turned herself in yet."

"I just left your mom and your brother. Mom looks ecstatic and Jordan looks good. When is your dad going to tell Jordan about Damon?"

"He said when he gets a little stronger," Jaylen replied.

"Well, I gotta go. Also, when you get home, can you check the lock on the front door? It looks like it has been tampered with."

I ran to the mall and picked up several gift cards to my mother's favorite stores. I stopped by Sweet Eats and ordered a beautiful birthday cake and a separate cake to welcome Marcus to our family. I also grabbed a gift card for Marcus in the amount of two hundred dollars from Foot Locker.

Tomorrow was going to be a busy day. We had to go to church and then rush home to get ready for Mom's birthday party. I need to call Gi'ana to make sure she had got the rest of the party items. I made my way back home, and then I called Roc and thanked him for everything. He told me that he was whipping up something special for dinner for Faith tonight. I told him not to keep her out all night, because she had church tomorrow. I wanted to spend a quiet evening with Jaylen, but Faith was adamant about stopping by to talk. I was able to relax for about an hour before Faith showed up. After she showed up, Jaylen went up to the hospital.

"Hey, girl. I told you that I was coming. Something is going on with you, and my gut tells me that it is serious," Faith declared.

"Faith, what I have to tell you has to stay between us. After you hear this, you are not going to know what to think," I replied.

"I'm waiting."

"The other night I came home and poured myself some merlot. I had two glasses because I needed to take the edge off. Anyway, before I know it, I pass out, and I start having this horrible dream that someone is raping me. I am pleading with them to stop, but I can't do anything, because I am too weak. It seemed like it was never going to end. Jaylen comes home two hours later and wakes me up. Now for it to be a dream, I shouldn't feel anything, right?"

"Right, Joi. So did you feel anything?"

"Hell yeah. My entire body was sore, including my private area. So what is your take?"

"Whoa. Give me a damn minute. Joi, I truly believe that you were raped, but how did someone get inside of your home? Do you still have any more wine left? Because if you do, we can go and have a sample analyzed."

"I found a possible piece of evidence in the bed," I revealed.

I ran into the kitchen to pour a glass of merlot into a small jar.

Jar in hand, I met Faith at the door.

"Well, hopefully, it was a pubic hair," Faith said.

"How did you know?"

"Because I just do. I studied all that shit in nursing school. Look, we have to get to the bottom of this. Have you made a doctor's appointment yet? Who would do something like this to you?"

"Damon. I mean, he is a career rapist. I also forgot to tell you that my front door looked like it had been tampered with."

"I will take a sample of the wine to work tomorrow and see if the lab can detect anything."

"Look, Faith, you are the only one who knows. Until I figure all of this out, you can't tell a soul."

"I think you should tell Jaylen," Faith asserted.

"I will once I get all the facts. I have to be sure. Suppose I am just so stressed out that it was a figment of my imagination?"

"I doubt it. I hear about this kind of shit all the time. I could just tell that something was wrong. Joi, I really hate that you are going through all this. You don't deserve it, but just ask God to pray for you tomorrow in church."

"Thanks for listening. I needed to tell my best friend. I feel a little better now."

"That will be one hundred fifty dollars for the session." Faith chuckled.

"I didn't ask you to come over here. You invaded my business."

"Cute. Well, I have to go. Are you going to be all right?"

"Yes," I assured her.

"Make sure you guys get the door fixed. Oops, I almost forgot. I need for you to put some of that wine in a container for me."

"Thanks for the reminder. I will be right back."

"I should know something in a couple of days."

"Here you go, and thanks again for stopping by."

"No problem. I see that your husband just pulled up, so take care, said Faith."

"Love you."

"Love you too."

Chapter 20

A Lot to Celebrate!

Joi

The next day was Sunday. That morning I met up with Faith and Taj as we parked in the parking lot of the church. This church was huge. We had to go and sit up in the balcony, but because they had so many flat-screen televisions, we could see everything. The chorus started the service off by singing a few songs. The pastor spoke briefly, and then he introduced a guest speaker. The guest speaker started preaching about relationships, which was right up my alley. After he spoke, they performed a mini play onstage about a woman making decisions in her life about talking to Jesus or taking her own life. She chose Jesus. Afterward, there was a selection by the praise team. They danced off of John P. Kee's new selection "I Worship Him." They gave me chills. Taj and Faith both were on their feet most of the service. I started to complete the form to make a donation to the church. The pastor came up to the podium and started preaching a sermon that was out of this world. He had me standing up. I knew that I had to bring Jaylen over to visit this church because of the atmosphere. Women, men, and children got saved, and so many people went up for prayer, including me.

After church was over, we left and I went home. I wanted to get ready because Vanessa was bringing Marcus to the house at 2:00 p.m.

"Jaylen? We have to leave to go over Mom's house in a few," I said when I walked inside the house.

"I will be ready in a few minutes. How was church?" Jaylen called.

"Awesome. I needed it so bad."

Jaylen and I wanted to get to my mother's home early. I had taken the liberty of inviting a few of our relatives. Gi'ana would be there, of course, and my niece Sharees.

We set up all the food and cake. Some more relatives stopped by to say happy birthday. Mom was so happy, and my father was just as happy. I looked out the window, and I could see Vanessa, Robert, and Marcus step out of the car. They rang the doorbell, and I ran over to answer it.

"Who is it, Joi?" Mom asked.

"It's your birthday present," I replied.

"Well, then, show me," Mom urged.

"Dad, can you please go over there by Mom? This present is for you, too," I said.

I signaled to Marcus and Vanessa to walk into

the room, and there were a few gasps. I looked over at my mother and father, and they sat there in pure shock.

"Young man, do I know you?" Dad asked.

"I'm not sure. I hope so," Marcus replied in a shy manner.

"Mom and Dad, I wanted to share some good news with you, and it has to do with Marcus," I announced. "I don't know any other way to explain it to you other than that Marcus is Wil's son."

"My Wil?" Mom whispered.

"Yes, Mom. Vanessa was pregnant with Wil's son at the time of his death. In a nutshell, she had to leave town to start over, and now she is back. Marcus wanted to meet everyone," I explained.

"Oh, Lord, somebody help me," Mom gasped. "I can't believe my eyes or my ears. Come here and give your grandmom and your grandpop a hug."

Mom started hugging Marcus, and she started crying. I hadn't seen my father cry in a long time, but he cried today. It was like a heavy burden had been lifted. Dad stood there and just stared at Marcus.

"Son, would you like something to drink?" Dad asked.

"Yes, sir," said Marcus.

"Yes, sir? Boy, call me Pop. Did anybody ever tell you that you look just like your father?" said Dad.

"That's what I am hearing," replied Marcus.

"Well, he looks identical to Wil at that age, and my heart is telling me that he is his son," Mom declared. "Marcus, welcome to our family, and come and give your grandmother another hug and kiss."

"Hey, don't forget your aunties," I added.

Tears continuously flowed down the faces of Mom and Dad. The rest of the family waited patiently to meet Wil's son. I could see a little more life pumped back into my parents by meeting Marcus. Vanessa stood to the side, alongside her husband. She seemed to be pleased. My mother got up and went to go and give Vanessa a hug. They snapped a lot of pictures with Marcus, and he seemed to enjoy every minute of it. Some of the family recognized Marcus from the newspapers as a local basketball superstar. Dad started showing Marcus photo albums of his father and told him that he would make some copies of videotapes of Wil's basketball games.

Now I felt like we could all move on.

"So, Mom, did you like your presents?" I asked just before leaving.

"Yes, Joi, and although everything was just so nice, the best present I received was finding out that I had a grandson from Wil. The second surprise was meeting him. Thank you so much. God is so good, and this is the best birthday ever!"

Chapter 21

Eboni's Return

Joi
A week later.

It was Saturday, and our girl Eboni had been away on the West Coast, developing her first rap artist for her father's record company. Well she was back now, and I would not miss her industry party for the world. Jaylen was supposed to come, but Jordan had come home yesterday, and Jaylen wanted to spend some quality time with him. On Friday Faith and Roc had had a nice evening, from what I heard, and Taj had spent some time with Orlando. So tonight was ladies' night. I had the perfect dress to wear to this industry party, and I couldn't wait to rock it tonight. I needed to call Eboni right away.

Ring. Click.

"Eboni? Hey, girl. It's me, Joi. What in the hell is up?"

"Girl, I know it's you. I'm just letting it do what it do," said Eboni.

"Is that some Westside slang or something?"

"Are you ready for the party tonight? You do know that it is an all-black affair?"

"You never mentioned that to me earlier," I replied.

"Joi, that's showbiz, so get with the program."

"Whoa, Eboni. I know you probably think you are Missy Elliott or Puff Mommy, but you are the same chick who just left the East Coast a couple of months ago. So please kill the swag, because you know that does not work for me."

"Oh, now you can't take a joke. What's up? I'm just having some fun."

"Eboni, please. While you were off in L.A. with your new thirty-plus-year-old rap artist—emphasis on *thirty plus*—we were here dealing with tons of drama."

"What drama? How come nobody called me to fill me in?" Eboni asked.

"Because we didn't want you to worry."

"Girl, I needed some scoop, and you guys held back on me. Now, tell me, but just make a long story short, because I have a hair appointment."

"Okay, long story short. Damon is in jail, Toni knows Damon, Faith's patient is Damon's mother, Wil has a son named Marcus, Jordan was in an accident, and brace yourself, because Jaylen is Damon's half brother and Faith is dating Roc."

"Hold up and back the hell up. Faith is dating who?"

"Roc. Is that all you are concerned about?" I grumbled.

"Well, yeah, but I had my eyes set on Roc, and she knew that shit."

"Hey, Roc can't sit around waiting for you."

"Girl, you are so right, but we are going to definitely have to talk, because all that shit you just ran down for me is deserving of making a long story long. I will hook up with you later tonight. I left three VIP tickets for you guys at the door. Signed, sealed, and delivered."

"Thanks, Eboni. I am so proud of you. My girl is doing her thing."

"I'm trying to. I want to be like you when I grow up," Eboni joked.

"We are only a week apart in age."

"Girl, I have to go. I am already late for my appointment."

I hung up with Eboni and quickly called Taj and Faith. I told them about Eboni's dress code. They were pissed just like me but happy about the VIP tickets at the door. I told them that she had left three tickets and not to bring anybody extra. And although I wouldn't be able to wear the dress I really wanted to wear, I still had a black dress that I could wear. I decided to call Vanessa to see how my nephew was doing. Marcus told me that he was staying over for the weekend because he was going fishing with his pop-pop. I couldn't wait to get on my father; he couldn't wait for this opportunity. Marcus said that his grandmother had not stopped baking him cookies, brownies, and cakes. They were already getting their basketball shirts with TAYLOR on the back, and the season had not even started yet. Marcus said that he had seen a lot of pictures of his dad and had read a lot of articles about him. Marcus could not believe the resemblance between him and his father, Wil. I told him not to eat all that junk, because it was important that he stayed in shape for the season. Jaylen and I couldn't wait to spend some quality time with him, as long as we could steal him from my parents for a few.

I ran to the local hair salon to see if they took walk-ins, and they did. Luckily, it was not that crowded, so I was able to get in a chair within minutes. My hair was finished in an hour, tops, and that was also a miracle in and of itself. I just got my hair washed, blow-dried, and flat ironed. They got me in and out. My next stop was the nail shop so that I could get a manicure, a pedicure, and my eyebrows waxed. It was somewhat crowded in the shop, but I decided to wait. Eventually, they called me over to the pedicure station. It took the nail tech about ninety minutes to complete everything. I knew I wasn't going to have enough time to make Jaylen dinner, but I wanted to see what he wanted to eat.

Ring. Click.

"Hey, beautiful," Jaylen said.

"Hi, baby. I miss you so much."

"I'm missing you, too, but promise me that we

will spend some time tomorrow, because I miss my wife."

"And I miss my husband."

"What time are you leaving for the party?" Jaylen asked.

"It starts at six and it's over at twelve midnight."

"Wake me up when you get in."

"No problem. Well, I have to run home and start getting ready, but I wanted to call you to see what you wanted to eat for dinner tonight."

"Don't worry your pretty little head over me," Jaylen insisted.

"Come on, Jay. Tell me, and I will run out and get it. I will drop it off at your mother's house, and I will make sure that it is enough for everybody."

"Well, that won't be necessary, because Mom has been cooking everything under the sun. She fried chicken and pork chops, baked macaroni and cheese, and she cooked string beans. She is so happy that Jordan is home, she can't sit down."

"Wow, she sounds like my mom," I mused. "She has turned into Betty Crocker. She has baked everything under the sun for Marcus. I think it's cute because she is so happy."

"Well, we are about to watch some sports, so I will be home waiting for you when you get home. I love you."

"I love you, too, Jaylen."

I hung up and hurried up home. I had a couple of hours to get myself ready. I told Taj and Faith that I would meet them there just in case I needed to leave early. I jumped into the shower and got dressed as fast as I could. I put on a little make-up and sprayed on some perfume. I could not make up my mind about what shoes I would wear, but eventually I decided to go with the silver heels. I gave myself a final glance. I didn't want to look available, yet I did not want to look frumpy. I was very pleased with my final opinion. So I grabbed my black purse, keys, and a few extra necessities, like gum. I set our alarm and then left the house.

I made my way to the location of the industry party. I valet parked my vehicle and went inside. People had already started filling the room. I looked around to see if I could find someone famous, but I didn't see anyone yet. I went over to the front door to get my ticket, and mines was the only one left, so that meant that Faith and Taj must have gone inside already, which was good. I started walking around to see if I could locate them, but I could not. I decided to go refresh my make-up, and that was when I bumped into Faith and Taj.

"Girl, I saw Beanie Seagal and Master P," Taj bragged.

"Well, I heard that Bow Wow and Snoop Dogg was coming," Faith replied.

"Where is Eboni? She has not seen us in a minute, and she is incognito," I said.

"Has anybody talked to Eboni since she got back?" asked Faith.

"I did," Taj said.

"Me too. Did you check out the West Coast slang?" I asked.

Taj nodded. "Yeah, I did, but I think that she has just been around those rappers for so long that she has just started talking like some of them." Taj laughed.

"As long as she doesn't start saying 'ya' mean' or 'true dat, true dat,'" I openly stated in a sarcastic tone.

"Eww, Joi, that is so two thousand two," Taj retorted.

"No. I got one. West-siyeeed!" Faith squealed.

"Faith, never say that again. That was horrible." I said.

"Enough of this. Let's go get some champagne." Taj suggested.

We headed for the bar and got three glasses of champagne. We wanted to do a toast with Eboni, but she was not available. We started mingling with some of the guests.

"Ooh, there goes Eve. Why does she have on red? I thought it was an all-black affair." Faith asked.

"Girl, you are not Eve. She can wear what she wants. That's one of the perks for being a celebrity." I explained as if I was a fashion guru.

"Hey, bitches. What's up?" Eboni yelled.

"We know that is probably Hollywood, but don't call us that. Seriously. You have lost your mind," Faith chided.

"Whatever, Faith, and what's this I hear that you are seeing my future baby's daddy, Roc?" said Eboni.

"Did she say baby's daddy?" Faith mumbled.

"Yes, she did." I said while rolling my eyes in the air.

"I'm just playing. I am glad that you wore black, or it would have been a problem," Eboni snarled.

"Well, why does Eve get a free pass with her red gown on?" Faith said in a demanding manner.

"Do you really have to ask? She is not common folk. Well, I am about to introduce my new artist, so go and get your VIP seats. I love you guys," Eboni said.

"Wow, it's worse than I thought. She is common and ghetto," Taj responded when Eboni walked away.

Eboni took the stage in preparation to introduce her new artist. We took our champagne and found our VIP section. The seats were not too bad. We decided to stand because people were already standing on their chairs. I was so busy looking around for some stars that I did not even realize that Eboni had taken the stage. I saw my telephone blinking, and I dialed in to check my new messages. One was from my ob-gyn's office.

"Hello, Joi. This is Dr. Hines, and I wanted to discuss two things with you. First of all, congratulations. You and the hubby are having a baby. Secondly, I need to schedule another appointment with you. I need to examine you again, so please don't forget to call me."

I'm pregnant. What if it turns out that I was actually raped by Damon? What am I going to do? Wow, this is too much to absorb, I screamed inside myself.

Just then Eboni began to speak. "Ladies and

gentlemen, I am honored to present to you a new artist under our record label. No doubt he is a hustler and a hard worker. He has been around the game for a minute, so he is no stranger to the stage. Most of his music went underground, but now we want to give you a little taste of the style and versatility that this rapper brings. I introduce to you S'Mack Down and his beautiful wife, Kendal."

As Eboni announced the name of her new artist, I slowly turned around. As soon as she finished saying his wife's name, I dropped my glass of champagne. He might be a rapper now, but I only remembered him and his slimy wife, Kendal, as the two people who had murdered my brother Will.

"I can't believe this! Had I known that this was the artist she was developing, I would not have wasted my damn time," I blurted out.

"Joi, please don't tell me that you know Eboni's artist," Taj said while looking confused.

"You damn right she knows that slimy piece of shit. He murdered her brother, Wil, years ago and got away with it," Faith snapped.

"I'm so sorry, Joi. I knew that your brother was murdered, but you never told me the murderer's name," said Taj.

"That's because I didn't want to talk about it," I replied.

It was obvious that Eboni didn't have a clue because after she introduced S'Mack Down or whatever his stupid name is, she came over to us like it was all good.

"So, ladies, what do you think of my new artist?" Eboni asked as she approached her three friends.

"We think that he is a murderer," Faith snapped.

"Yeah, whatever. Just stop with all the hate, Faith. I'm sure your little nursing career is going to take off one day," Eboni hissed.

Faith rolled her eyes.

"I'm not even going to respond to that, considering that the only skill you have is being Daddy's little girl."

"C'mon, Faith and Taj. I really do not want to hear this right now. I have to go," I said.

"Wait, Joi. I will come with you," Taj replied.

"What is going on? What is this all about?" Eboni snapped.

"Like I tried to tell you a minute ago, that rapper of yours murdered Joi's brother when he was dating Kendal," Faith answered.

"Oh, my gosh. Joi, I am so sorry. I didn't know. You know that I would never do anything in this world to hurt you, I never knew his name. I have to go." Eboni said.

I sighed. "Eboni, don't worry about it. I know you didn't know. This is just too painful for me. I hope that you understand why I need to leave."

"I do. I will call you later this evening to check on you," Eboni promised.

Eboni slowly walked back toward the stage. I could tell that she was blown away by the news about her new artist's past. I felt bad for her, but I felt worse being confronted with the man who had killed my brother. He didn't deserve a career,

because he took Wil's life and career away when
he pulled the trigger. Kendal had the nerve to
be hanging on to his arm like the dutiful wife. I
should have walked up on that stage and slapped
the shit out of her. She had played my brother to
the end. Kendal had known what had happened,
but she'd refused to come clean, and as a result,
Mack had got away with murder. As far as I was
concerned, she'd murdered Wil, too.

As I walked out of the building, I could hear
S'Mack Down's rap music playing in the background. Even if I didn't know him, I wouldn't have
bought his music, because it was wacked.

Ring.

"Hello?" I said.

"Hey, Joi. It's me, Jaylen. Look, can you come
down to the police station? They have several sus-
pects who may have been working with Damon."

"On my way." I somberly agreed.

"Joi, are you okay? How was the party?"

"It's just too much to talk about right now. I'm
glad I left."

"Are you sure you are up to this? We can do this
tomorrow."

"No, Jay. I need to hopefully bring some closure to my life before I completely lose it."

As I drove to the police station, Eboni called to
check on me. She told me that she was breaking
S'Mack Down's contract with their record company
because he failed to disclose this information. She
said that she knew he was a thug, but because of our
friendship, she just could not continue to support

someone who murdered my brother. In her mind, I was like a sister, so in a way he murdered her damn brother. I had mixed emotions, because I know how hard Eboni worked on this project, but at the end of the day that is what true friends do. I would have done the same thing for her.

Chapter 22

Jail or Hell

Toni

As I pulled into the police station, I took a few minutes to get myself together and reflect on everything that had happened in the last two years. I had made some bad decisions, and now I was going to have to deal with the consequences. The one thing I regretted the most was losing my son. He was the only thing that made sense in my life. The courts had given Kenyatta temporary custody because I left little K.J. in the car and went shopping for some shoes at DSW. I honestly forgot he was in the car, and it was also eighty-five degrees outside. A woman walked by and saw my baby crying, and she called the police. Shortly thereafter, the police and the ambulance arrived. They were able to get the car door open and take the baby out, unbeknownst to me. As I headed toward my car, all I saw were police vehicles and an ambulance, along with a slew of spectators. I had no idea what was going on, so I ran toward my car, and when I saw little K.J. in the care of the EMT, I freaked out. I told the officer that it was my car and that the baby was mine. He pulled me over to the side and started asking me a lot of questions. I tried to explain to him that I had honestly forgot K.J. was in there. I pleaded with the officer to let me go with my baby to the hospital, and he finally agreed.

I called Kenyatta and explained everything to him. His friend took him to get our car from the parking lot, and he came up to the hospital. I was in the examination room when he barged in to see little K.J. I knew something was wrong by the way he looked at me. We were in the emergency room for about an hour before they released my son. I asked Kenyatta what was the matter, and he asked me if I had been smoking a blunt this morning. At that point, I knew where he was going with it. I told him that I had taken only a few hits. After that, he just went off. He told me that he had seen the weed in the ashtray. He said that I was a fucked-up individual and a bad mother. He was so mad at me that he took K.J. and left for a couple of days. I called him every day, and he accused me of being high and forgetting the baby because I was irresponsible. Kenyatta broke off the relationship and told me that he was seeking full custody of little K.J. I begged him to forgive me, but he refused. He told me that if I made it an issue, he would tell the authorities everything and that I would not see my baby ever again. Every now and then, I got to see him. I just hoped and prayed that Kenyatta and little K.J. would forgive me. I knew my son would be better with me, but now I felt like maybe he was better without me.

I knew that marrying Jaylen was a mistake, because he still loved Joi, and I would never measure up to her, and I took that shit personal. Everybody thought she was so perfect, and I took that shit personal, too. Hell, who could measure up to this chick? When she showed up at my wedding, I was livid. Here was this beautiful, well-dressed, highly sophisticated, educated attorney, and she was the love of Jaylen's life. I mean, his parents adored her to the point where there was barely anything left for me. How dare she sashay her ass all up into my wedding day, trying to outshine me? I wanted to think of myself as beautiful, educated, and smart, too. I was not a bad catch. The only person I could talk to was Jordan. He accepted me as his sister-in-law from day one. I didn't have to measure up to him. I just prayed that he was all right; I needed to call the hospital to check on his condition.

Ring.

"Hello, Cooper Medical. How may I help you?"

"Can you please transfer me to patient information?"

"Hold on, please."

"Hello. Patient information. May I please have

the patient's name and room number?" the operator asked.

"Uh, yes, his name is Jordan Payne."

"Are you immediate family?"

"I used to be his sister-in-law."

"I'm sorry. We can only give patient information to immediate family."

"So you can't tell me if he is better or if he was discharged?"

"I'm sorry. We are unable to give out that information." The operator advised her.

Those freakin' hospitals got on my nerves. Everything was top secret. If I had the time, I would go up there and demand to speak with someone in charge. But they might just throw my ass out.

"What am I going to do? What am I going to do? Damn you, Damon." I said aloud.

I always wanted to meet him when he was playing for the Philadelphia Eagles. Once I met him, I realized that he was a calculating sociopath. Now it was time for me to turn myself in, because I had nowhere else to go.

"Hello. May I please speak to someone in charge?"

"How can I help you?" the officer asked.

"I'm here to turn myself in," I sobbed.

"Toni, what are you doing? For your own sake, you'd better be turning yourself in," Joi asked as Toni approached her from the other side of the lobby.

"I'm sorry, Joi, for everything that I have ever done to you," I said. "As much as I hated you, I was wrong. Now I have to pay the price. I have been working with Damon to destroy you and Jaylen. I knew he was trying to hurt Jaylen, but Jordan got in the way, and now he is fighting for his life. I just pray that he pulls through. I tried to find out about his condition from the hospital but they refused to tell me because I'm not family. I will never forgive myself for that because Jordan is the only one who ever cared about me when I was in the family. I tried to write bad checks against Jaylen's account. I lost my son because I was too damn stupid."

"Toni? Don't say another word," Damon said.

I looked up, and the police were escorting Damon through the station. He was handcuffed, but he was ordering me not to say anything else. I looked over to my right, and there was Jaylen. He was holding on to Joi.

"Shut up, Damon," I snarled. "Please back away from me, or I will shoot you and the officer. Oh yeah, Joi, and you're going to love this part. That night you thought you were dreaming, you weren't. Damon and I were already in your house, and he managed to put that date-rape drug in your wine. He raped you, and I watched until I could not watch anymore. I did plead with him to stop, but he wouldn't. I finally just left the room, because he kept yelling at me."

"Bitch, shut up, or you will regret it," Damon yelled.

"There's nothing more you can do. You ruined my life, and now I have nothing to live for," I shouted. "You put me out there and admitted to my face that you were only using me! You piece of shit! I *hate* you, Damon! You're a *monster*, and I hope you rot in hell!"

"You raped my wife! I'm going to kill you Damon! I'm going to kill you both!" Jaylen screamed.

"Jay, please. She has lost it and none of us may make it out of here alive," Joi pleaded. "Toni, please put the gun down. Jordan is okay, so don't worry. We can talk about this."

"Oh yeah right, me talk to you. Bitch, please. My competition. You have been nothing but a pain in my ass from day one. But since you want to be the hero, bring your ass over here so I can show you how I feel every day, which is scared."

Joi slowly started walking over toward me, and Jaylen grabbed her. The police officer yelled at her to get back, because I was dangerous.

"Jay, let me go. I got this," Joi said.

"The hell you do," Jaylen snapped.

"Step back Jay, I don't want to hurt you but I will," I said, while pointing the gun at Damon.

"Miss, please put the gun down or I'm afraid that I am going to have to shoot you," the officer threatened.

"I'm the fuckin' victim here. Don't you see that!" I screamed.

"Toni, please let me help you. I forgive you," Joi begged.

"Yeah right. So what are you going to do, super-hero?" I laughed.

Joi continued to walk over to me. I pointed the

gun at her for a second, and I saw Damon move. I quickly aimed the gun at Damon and shot his ass three times. Afterward, I aimed the gun at myself and pulled the trigger, because I'd rather go to hell than jail.

Discussion Questions

1. Joi and Jaylen have been dealing with a lot of drama. Do you think that their marriage will last?
2. Why do Damon and Toni choose such a path for themselves?
3. Jaylen and Jordan's mother and father seem to have a great marriage, but what seems to be missing?
4. What role do you think the guy with the dreadlocks plays in this book?
5. Do you think that Joi was raped? If so, how do you think it might have happened?
6. Why was Faith so upset when she saw Tyree's wedding announcement?
7. Do you think it was too soon for Marcus to meet Joi's family on her mother's birthday?
8. If you could change the title of this book, what would you call it?
9. What do you think about Roc and Faith hooking up?
10. Do you think Joi's constant paranoia is going to pull her and Jaylen apart?

Roslyn Wyche-Hamilton is originally from Neptune, NJ. She is married and has two beautiful children. Roslyn Wyche-Hamilton graduated from Delaware State University with a dual degree in Accounting and Business Administration. She is a member of Delta Sigma Theta Sorority. After working in Corporate America for many years she changed careers in 2002. In 2005, she graduated with a master's degree in Education (School Leadership) from Wilmington University. She is currently scheduled to graduate with another master's degree in Human Resources in 2009. Her plans are to reach out to others who desire to write and help them through the process.